P9-DXL-343

ALWAYS

HAPPY

HOUR

ALWAYS
HAPPY
HOUR

STORIES

MARY
MILLER

LIVERIGHT PUBLISHING CORPORATION

A Division of W. W. Norton & Company
Independent Publishers Since 1923

New York | London

For information about permission to reproduce selections from this book,
write to Permissions, Liveright Publishing Corporation, a division of
W. W. Norton & Company, Inc., 500 Fifth Avenue, New York, NY 10110

For information about special discounts for bulk purchases, please contact
W. W. Norton Special Sales at specialsales@wwnorton.com or 800-233-4830

Manufacturing by LSC Communications
Book design by Chris Welch
Production manager: Louise Mattarelliano

ISBN 978-1-63149-218-1

Liveright Publishing Corporation
500 Fifth Avenue, New York, N.Y. 10110
www.wwnorton.com

W. W. Norton & Company Ltd.
15 Carlisle Street, London W1D 3BS

1 2 3 4 5 6 7 8 9 0

For my exes

Thanks to the editors of the following journals, where earlier versions of these stories first appeared: "The House on Main Street" in *The Austin Review*; "At One Time This Was the Longest Covered Walkway in the World" in *Fiction*; "Big Bad Love" in *The Good Men Project*; "Uphill" in *Mississippi Noir Anthology*; "Dirty" in *Sententia*; "He Says I Am a Little Oven" in *Mid-American Review*; "Love Apples" in *Indiana Review*; "Hamilton Pool" in *Fiction*; "Always Happy Hour" as "Always Happy Hour, Always Summer" in *American Short Fiction*; "Little Bear" in *Mississippi Review*; "Charts" in *Story*; "The 37" in *Joyland*.

CONTENTS

The parking lot after a movie is the broken open world.

—Mark Leidner,
"Love in the Time of Whatever Disease This Is"

INSTRUCTIONS

He leaves her a series of drawings on a sheet of typing paper. It must have taken him a long time—he probably got off to a late start. She only wanted to know the code to the laundry room, where his mailbox key is.

She lies in bed with his cats, studying it. At the top, there is a banner like the kind waving behind an airplane, advertising two-for-one drink specials at the beach: *In the event of my unlikely death,* and underneath it a headstone: *Everything Was Beautiful and Nothing Hurt.* There's a single flower next to the headstone, a few wisps of grass. There are boxes labeled GATOS, COFFEE, PAR AVION, BASURA, and one with nothing but a question mark. In the box labeled PAR AVION, he tells her that the mail key is hanging next to the brass knuckles. The GATOS section takes up most of the left side. There's a diagram of a litter box showing how the pee clumps and advising her to scoop at least twice a day so the cats "don't get weird." BASURA . . . in the parking lot.

Does he think she's incapable of taking out the trash and feeding some cats?

She gets out of bed and goes to the kitchen to drink the last of his coffee, which is cold, so she puts ice cubes in it, milk and sugar. She stirs it with a clean spoon and places the spoon in the sink. *Everything was beautiful and nothing hurt,* she thinks, standing there in her socks.

She opens his cabinets to look at the same things that are always in his cabinets and which are entirely more interesting than the things in her own. There are still plenty of candy bars that his aunt brought back from New Zealand, frogs on the wrappers. There are Tic Tacs and many bottles of olive oil and spices from the Mediterranean grocery. Above his refrigerator, four boxes of cereal. She will eat cereal and candy bars and pick up sandwiches from Little Deli. She'll ride his stationary bike while watching *The Office* and *Girls.* Already, she misses her apartment with all of her books, and her balcony where she can smoke without the old ladies watching her, the cats gazing at her from their perch.

She finishes her coffee and puts the cup in the sink next to the spoon. Despite the COFFEE box, and the instructions therein (just YouTube CHEMEX, filters above sink), she won't drink it at his house. He has too many ways of making it, all of which seem unnecessarily difficult and time-consuming.

She puts her shoes back on and tells the cats goodbye. She likes these cats only because they are his, because their presence makes them more like a family. They creep around the apartment at night searching for something to knock over, wake her up early to eat. When she's reading in bed, they stick their nails into the pages of her book one at a time and pause to observe her reaction.

She drives to work thinking about the things she knows that have hurt him: his cousin's death, broken bones, the time he swallowed a bunch of pills and drank too much vodka because he was young and overseas. She thinks about the things that have hurt her and then she thinks about beauty and how little of it she sees in even beautiful things. She wonders if people who've been hurt more see more beauty. She wonders how a few strung-together words can seem so meaningful when she doesn't believe them at all.

At lunch, she texts her boyfriend to ask if he wrote it.

It's from *Slaughterhouse-Five*, he texts back.

Of course it is. It's the kind of thing hipsters tattoo on their arms—The heart is a lonely hunter, Not all who wander are lost, Everything was beautiful and nothing hurt.

She's disappointed but should have caught the allusion.

A few hours later, she's back at his apartment. She accepts a stack of coupons from his next-door neighbor as she unlocks the door.

"Thank you," she says. "This is great."

The woman seems disappointed; she isn't as effusive, as excited, as she should be. "Those are free," the woman says, "the best barbeque sandwich in town."

She thanks the woman again and tells her she'll definitely use them.

"If you're not going to use them, just give them back."

"I'll definitely use them," she repeats, as she closes the door and locks it. She draws the blinds, turns on all the lights.

She throws the coupons away. She doesn't like barbeque, how everyone is always talking about the best barbeque in the city. She has never waited in a long line at Franklin's, surrounded by people in lawn chairs sipping from to-go cups, or driven miles and miles out into the country to go to some obscure shack for something more authentic.

She scoops out the litter box and feeds the cats, studies the drawings again—if she's reading it correctly, her boyfriend feeds them four times a day, a steady stream of food in their shared bowl. Tomorrow she'll do better. At the bottom of the paper there are hearts—six of them—and three Love You's . . . She considers the difference between *Love you* and *I love you*. *Love you* is what she tells her friends when she has to get off the phone abruptly or cancel plans. In this case, she feels he used *Love you* because it looked better, which is something her boyfriend is always conscious of—everything carefully considered and thought out. She decided a long time ago she didn't want to be a careful person, that she didn't want to live her life constantly worrying about what other people thought of her. Of course she *does* worry, she does nothing but worry, and all her lack of care amounts to is that she offends people constantly and tests them with her inappropriateness and expects them to love her for it.

She drags around a feather on a stick, turns to look at the cats: they stare at her without blinking or averting their gaze. She puts the feather in the male's face, drops it to his nose, and he paws at it a few times before giving up. She kneels and crooks her finger at them like her boyfriend does. They come forward to bump her with their foreheads and she gets into bed, feels the small hairs tickling her face. They climb around her purring, louder and louder, and she wonders if she could put them in her car and take them to her apartment. Cats don't travel well, she recalls her boyfriend saying. They scream and shit everywhere.

She has no pets, has never had a pet, and her boyfriend was sorry for her when she told him. She didn't tell him that her family was poor, that she'd collected frogs and snakes and turtles from her backyard, which she'd let die in jars and shoeboxes. She'd once put half a dozen frogs in a doll-house her mother had bought at a garage sale, closed it up and watched them through the windows. Of course he knows she grew up poor. When you grow up poor, even if you do everything thereafter to be not-poor, there's no way to shake it completely. She likes to read about lottery winners, how desperately they go about losing everything so they can get back to the state at which they are familiar.

She looks at her open suitcase on the floor, her purse and backpack and tennis shoes. Her MacBook Pro, only a few months old. The other times she's been at his apartment without him, she was waiting for him to come home—he was going to show up at any minute and they would have sex and watch movies and scratch each other's backs. They would talk and laugh.

She walks over to his closet and takes out the leather coat that cost him seven hundred dollars, tries it on. It barely zips. Her boyfriend is small. She puts her hands in the pockets:

empty. She's always asking him how much things cost, how much he paid, and he hates this about her. She knows he hates this about her but it only makes her do it more.

In the event of my untimely death, she thinks—no, not untimely—*unlikely.*

She picks up the male, also smaller than his female counterpart, the one she has decided she likes least. The cat struggles and then allows her to carry him into the kitchen. She sets him down and takes the packet of treats off the counter, shakes it. It's full of dried bits that look just like their regular food. The female comes slinking into the kitchen as she pours the bits onto the floor saying, treat, treat.

When they have finished the bits and sauntered off, she opens the refrigerator, checks the expiration date on a container of cream cheese. It expired more than four months ago but the milk is good, as are the eggs. She makes herself a drink with his Uncle Val's, carries it into the bathroom and sets it on the counter while she pees, the female watching her from just outside the door. Though she and her boyfriend spend nearly every night together, she has never come upon any evidence that he does anything in the bathroom other than take a piss. The whole thing is very curious. She has begun to listen carefully, turn down the volume on the TV. She goes in there right after him to see if she can smell anything. Nothing—there is never anything.

The cat approaches her, warily, and knocks her razor off the edge of the bathtub. The blade pops off and she yells and the cat hightails it under the bed. She searches but can't find it; she is certain that the cat has swallowed it and this makes her feel miserable because her boyfriend knew she would need instructions; he knew she would fuck it up somehow.

She tries to lure the cat out from under the bed. She lifts one corner of the mattress and the cat moves to a safe area while the other watches. She moves from one corner to another, lifting the mattress as she looks for the blade, but it is nowhere. She gets back into bed and sips at her drink. When her boyfriend makes himself a cocktail at home, it always goes unfinished. He forgets about it until it's too watered down to drink and then pours it out. She wants to see if she can do this: a test. If she doesn't finish this drink, she will win. Other than the cats, the only other thing under the bed is a gun. Her boyfriend said it was loaded and the safety was off, that she shouldn't touch it unless she was prepared to use it. He showed her how to open the barrel and take the bullets out, but she forgot as soon as he put it away. It's like CPR class, no matter how many times she's certified, she wouldn't be able to save anyone's life.

Her boyfriend calls, says he is one hundred miles from lovely beautiful San Francisco.

Do you want to live with me in California one day? she asks.

We're going to crush California, kid, he says. We'll have the breeziest house with the biggest windows that face the sea. I'll bring you fresh-baked bread every morning and then get out of your hair.

When are you going to get your tattoo? she asks.

Tomorrow, he says.

Before he left, he went over each of his tattoos with her, telling her what they meant and why he'd gotten them. One of them says CARPET inside a human heart. It didn't always say CARPET—it was a girl's initials and his choices were limited. There are a lot of literary allusions. When he was young, he had a Gertrude Stein poem tattooed on his back but now it's covered up with a bull and bear fighting: the bull appears to be winning but he said that neither ever wins; they are perpetually locked in battle. There are references to Proust and Nabokov and L. Frank Baum. And then there are all of the small ones that remind her of her high school notebooks, the margins filled with stars and four-leaf clovers.

He likes her skin clean and white.

It's lonely here without you, she says. I brought *The Road* but I need you to read it to me. For weeks he has been reading *The Road* to her. As much as she likes it, she can't seem to read more than a page at a time because it is lulling and repetitive and so beautiful that it puts her in a kind of trance. Only when he reads it to her is she able to translate the words into images and the images into meaning. She opens the book to their place: *Crossing the grass he felt faint and he had to stop. He wondered if it was from smelling the gasoline.* She wants to figure out how sentences this simple add up to something she can't comprehend.

They talk for ten more minutes, all the while she is wondering whether to tell him that his cat has probably swallowed a razor blade and is going die. When she hears his voice change—he's ready to get off the phone—she tells him. The blade popped off, she says, and I can't find it. I think she may have swallowed it.

A cat wouldn't swallow a razor blade, he says, but she's not so sure. She is confused about what cats will and won't do. They don't get out of the way when she swings his kettlebells, for example, and one time she knocked the male in the head with a crack her boyfriend heard from the other room.

They say I love you and goodbye—I love you I love you goodbye—and it's quiet again. She's afraid her boyfriend will die in a car accident or will drunkenly fall down the stairs and break his neck. That she will never see him again. She turns on the TV and tries to find something to watch, thinking about the dream he had recently, how he woke her in the middle of the night to tell her about it: *we were in a boat and there was a great storm,* he said. *And I lost my oars so I paddled with my arms. And the piranhas ate my arms, chewed them down to nothing but I kept paddling. I kept paddling and paddling, trying to get us to shore.* And that was the end: her boyfriend paddling madly with his nubby arms in an attempt to save them. It was a dream about worry, she knows, as nearly all dreams are. He worries his love will run out. He loves her so much and it scares him because maybe their love isn't sustainable— perhaps they should each find someone they could love less. Or maybe she simply isn't the girl he thought she was, the one he wanted her to be. She has disappointed him. She has disappointed herself by disappointing him and she can't stop disappointing him because she's disappointed that he's disappointed and so on. Everything is fine, she told him, smoothing back his hair and taking hold of his arm. We're happy, she assured him. There are no great storms here.

THE HOUSE
ON MAIN STREET

On Wednesdays there's a farmers' market downtown. My roommate Melinda bikes the three blocks to Town Square Park and returns with a bag of deer sausage or a whole chicken. She's a small girl, about five feet tall with the tiniest shoes and panties I have ever seen, but she eats a lot. Other times, she brings home goat or dove or squirrel. She's also here to get her PhD, but she's from New York City and hates everything about this place except its strange meat and the proximity to New Orleans. I told her that my brothers used to hunt raccoons but they didn't eat them—they gave them away to black people. She said that was racist, but it's just the truth, that's what they did, and I don't really see how it's racist. Perhaps just something I shouldn't have mentioned.

I frequently feel compelled to confirm her worst suspicions of us because she's always saying it's too humid here and there are no dateable men, that people holler at her when she's jogging or riding her bike, all of which are things I hate as well, but she makes me feel like it's my fault. And where the fuck are the sidewalks? she asks me, as if I have personally decided that this town would be better off without them.

Today Melinda has brought home a chicken. She likes chicken best, boils the entire thing in a pot. I stand in the kitchen and look at it. The pot is full, the fat bird bobbing on the surface. I rarely eat meat now because I hate the bloody bags she carries up the stairs, leaking all over the place, and the flesh-colored bodies plucked clean. While her chicken boils, she has sex with a third-year PhD student, a guy who's struggling with his religious convictions. He is blond and tall, which is my type, but he's also Baptist and clean-cut and gets along well with everyone, which is not.

The water bubbles over, chicken fat getting everywhere. Melinda never cleans the stove. She's opposed to cleaning entirely, so far as I can tell, and because I didn't make the mess, I won't clean it either.

I'm tense whenever she's in the house, and the only way to ease this tension is by talking to her. She tells me how many pull-ups she can do, how the training is going for her next marathon. I ask about her poems, which are about apples and trees and never become more than apples and trees. I guess my main problem with her is that she doesn't seem to be afraid of anything.

I take a beer from the refrigerator and sit on the counter, look out the window that she leaves propped open with a wine bottle. There's a stray bottle out there on our flat roof, and I could easily climb out and pick it up, but it's been there so long it has become part of the scenery. My previous apartment had the best counter sitting, a recessed window that made me feel like I was tucked away where no one could see me. I lived there alone and everything was mine, but my divorce money has run out and my ex-husband doesn't think it's funny anymore when I call him up and ask him to send me a check. I am no longer his responsibility, which is a great relief to him. It's a great relief to me too. I don't want his money. It's like I was calling him up to ask for something he could never give me, was never able to give me, and was only doing it to offer him the opportunity to say no.

When I finish my beer, they're still at it. There is nothing more disgusting, really, than people enjoying themselves so thoroughly when you're miserable.

I toss my bottle cap, which I've been clutching so tightly there's a ring in the center of my palm, out the window and take the last beer from the refrigerator. The blond guy will have to leave soon to go to church, and this makes me feel a little better. I know he'll hate himself, and he'll hate her for making him hate himself. In half an hour he'll be staring at the back of the pretty church girl he likes who is dating someone else, someone stronger than he is, stronger than he could ever be. He'll look down at his wrinkled khakis and know he'll never have her.

I remove the bottle from the window and turn on the air conditioner. Then I call Ben, wake him from a nap. Ben does whatever I say because he's in love with me and sometimes I sleep with him. He always lets me initiate things, and I do it whenever I feel like what I owe him is more than I want to owe.

"Let's go drinking," I say. "I'm out of beer."

He says he's tired and hungover and then sighs and tells me to give him an hour. An hour is a reasonable amount of time so I agree. I'll have to shower and find something to wear. I'll have to put on some eyeliner and smudge concealer under my eyes. I know where we'll go, where we always go: the karaoke bar where people drink at every hour of the day. It's a dive but there's a jukebox with plenty of Johnny Cash and the toilets always flush and they don't care how drunk you get. Some places will kick you out if they see you fall off a barstool or fold your arms on the bar to have a catnap but not Shenanigan's.

The blond guy mumbles something, undershirt going over his head. Maybe he'll run home and make himself present-able before church. Maybe he'll punch himself in the chest and tell God how sorry he is for having sex with an atheist from New York City, once again, how he will stop, how he has already stopped because it was the very last time.

Instead of showering, I lie in bed staring at the tops of trees.

Our apartment takes up the entire second floor of an old colonial. We each have two large rooms and our own bath-room. We share a kitchen, a dining area, and a small alcove where our washer and dryer are stacked. A man and his dead lover's son live in the renovated space below—they don't like each other, but they each own half and it's a bad time to sell (according to Melinda). I listen for their raised voices, for any voices at all, but it's always so quiet down there. I imagine them eating and watching television in their house slippers, completely separate, as if the other does not exist.

Ben calls me from his car. I put on my favorite pair of jeans and a clean shirt, check my face in the mirror, and then stand on the toilet to check my body. I need new clothes and shoes. I have no idea how I'm managing to live off my graduate student assistantship—it is so little money—but I am. My peers take out loans so they can go to fancy dinners, buy dresses and high heels.

"Thanks for coming to get me," I say, settling myself into the passenger seat of his gray four-door sedan.

"No problem. Where do you want to go?"

"We're not going to play that game, are we?" I ask, flipping the ashtray closed.

"Well," he says.

Shenanigan's is less than three miles away but in a town this small that's far. I keep moving to smaller and smaller towns and the distances grow accordingly. Five miles used to be nothing. Now three seems excessive, ridiculous. And if it's cold or rainy out, forget it. My most recent ex-boyfriend grew up in Los Angeles and thought nothing of driving fifteen miles to eat sushi, which was one of the reasons it didn't work out between us. Not the distance, exactly, but the way distances framed our worlds.

"You sleep all day?" I ask.

"I stayed up last night."

"You were playing that video game again."

He opens the ashtray and lights a cigarette.

I've watched him play his game before; it's just a bunch of code, an indecipherable collection of numbers and signs that made me feel dumb so I made fun of it. And of course there's

THE HOUSE ON MAIN STREET

a girl on there he likes, a girl who lives a thousand miles away so he can imagine her beautiful and accommodating, so he can imagine they might fall in love.

We sit at the bar, the side closest to the bathroom and juke-box. Ben hands Michelle his debit card and she brings us two Miller Lites. I know he won't let me split the bill when it comes, but I don't feel too bad about it because even if we take shots it won't be more than thirty dollars.

"You want to play pool?" he asks.

"No way."

He goes to the bathroom while I drink my beer and try not to make eye contact with anyone. The other grad students only come on Thursdays because it's steak night: a slab of meat, a baked potato, and a salad for seven dollars.

When he returns, I tell him that I listened to Melinda have sex for an hour earlier, that I thought it would go on forever.

"Were you just standing outside her door?" he asks.

"Pretty much."

"How would you feel if she did that to you?"

"You don't like her, what do you care?"

"I just think it's rude," he says.

"People in New York share everything—they hang a cur-tain in the middle of a room and pretend they're alone."

Like Melinda, Ben is also a poet, but he doesn't write about fruit or trees. He writes about McRibs and factories and Walmart. He writes about me. There's a poem about the time I threw his I Ching at Crescent City, another about the afternoon we met at a Waffle House in Memphis and how he knew by the texture of my skin I'd slept with someone else. And then there's the one where I'm in my panties reading Don DeLillo while he makes lasagna. He gives me ways of seeing myself differently, provides me with images I wouldn't otherwise have. I wouldn't remember reading Don DeLillo in my panties, wouldn't remember any of the things he has deemed important. It's like I get to have my own memories and his too.

I rest a hand on his knee, my fingers searching out the hole in his jeans so I can feel his skin. A guy in a wheelchair rolls through the door. He looks at me and I look away because one time he told me I was the most beautiful girl he'd ever seen and I was embarrassed for both of us because I'm not that pretty, because he was only able to approach me in that way because I'd never be with him.

We order shots of whiskey and another round of beers, but when karaoke starts I ask him to take me home.

Ben pulls up to my house and we sit there for a minute with his car running. The basketball that's been rolling around in his trunk is finally still. As we kiss, I wonder what it would be like to want to fuck someone so badly you'd do it even though it goes against everything you truly desire.

I climb the stairs and find Melinda at the dining room table with a glass of red wine and a full plate: half a chicken, vegetables, and spinach in a separate bowl. She never allows herself more than one glass of wine and only with a meal.

"You're like a European," I say. "What time is it?"

"I don't know—nine? Ten? Where'd you go?" she asks, but I don't want to tell her. She would never go to Shenanigan's, would never be friends with Ben, and can't understand why

Ha onaintreet

would.nytimedate anyone at all, for even a minute, she tells me I'm too good for him.

In the morning, I listen to Melinda bang around: opening cabinets and slamming them, pots clanking. I can't believe how loud she is, how little regard she has for me. It is seven-thirty and already painfully bright outside. I need curtains but this seems completely beyond the realm of possibility—where would I get them and would they be long enough? I'd probably have to have them made. I watch the occasional big-winged bird fly by and think about what I have to do today. I don't have class until six. I have a few stories to read but that shouldn't take me longer than thirty or forty minutes. Despite my teaching schedule and three classes a semester, there is so much time.

I call my ex-husband. He picks up on the third ring. He always makes me wonder if he's going to pick up but he always does.

"What are you doing?" I ask.

"On my way to work," he says, taking a sip of something. And then he says, "Guess who died?"

"What?"

"Guess who died?"

"Mrs. White."

"Mrs. White already died."

"Oh yeah." She was old, ninety-seven or ninety-eight, our next-door neighbor. "Who then?"

"Jonah," he says.

"Jonah?"

"Jonah," he repeats. "One night he drank too much and didn't wake up." He sounds excited about it.

"Wait, what are you talking about?"

"He drank too much one night and didn't wake up."

Jonah was our closest friend, though I haven't seen or spoken to him since I left Meridian. I've hardly even thought of him because I've done my best to put everyone and everything in that town behind me. It hasn't been difficult. Once you leave a place like that, so long as it isn't your hometown, you know you won't ever have to see any of those people again.

"Jonah's dead?"

"Yeah."

"It's really messed up that you would tell me like this. Why didn't you call me? And why would you say it like that—*guess who died?*"

He explains that Jonah had been going downhill for the past year. He'd stopped coming over to the house; he hadn't even seen him in months.

"When?"

"Three or four weeks ago."

"Well this is all very upsetting."

"I'm sorry," he says, and then he doesn't say anything else so I hang up. I won't contact him again—there is no news he could give me that might make me glad I called. Jonah. *Jesus.* There was a time when I thought I might have been in love with him, though I was just unhappy and had wanted someone to do something about it and he'd been the likeliest candidate. I can see him in our kitchen with one of his girlfriends, an older divorced lady who didn't want to hang out with us so we'd been seeing him less frequently. They'd come from the tennis court, were wearing their tennis whites. I try to picture him at the Mexican restaurant we frequented or sitting next to me in a lawn chair while my ex grilled hamburgers, but I can't remember him with any specificity at any time or in any place other than this one. It makes me wonder how my closest friends will remember me when I'm gone— what completely insignificant moment will they recall?

He used to burn CDs for me, music he thought I'd like interspersed with the songs he'd written. I don't know where they are; there were so many and I had thought so little of them.

When I hear Melinda run down the stairs, I put on a pair of shorts and rummage around in my purse for a cigarette. Then I go outside and sit on the stoop. Across the street there's a crack house with a blue-tarp roof. I'm not sure how many people live there—a cast of characters come and go, cackling and drinking, tossing bottles into a trash can full of bottles: smash! But they're quiet now.

I unlock my car, check the console and glove box. I find one of Jonah's CDs in the passenger side door, still in its envelope with his small script: SONGS FOR L. I take it upstairs and download it to my computer, listen to "Rhinestone Lady," "Porno King from New Orleans," "Monkey Lover." The lyrics I used to think were funny now seem seriously fucked up, but the melodies are nice. I might have loved Jonah. But if I loved him, why haven't I thought of him? I imagine that I'm the one who might have saved him. For every man who commits suicide, there must be a dozen women who convince themselves that they were the only one with the power to save him and they failed.

In the kitchen, I take an energy bar out of the cabinet and chew it slowly, laboriously.

Melinda's doors are open—they're always wide open when she leaves. I walk into her bedroom and look at the comforter on the floor and the piles of books scattered about. A couple of wooden fish hang from the ceiling; brightly colored tapestries are tacked to the walls. There's a medal from a marathon and half a dozen framed pictures on her dresser. I only have two pictures in the apartment: an elementary school photo of my sister, back when she was thin-limbed and straight-haired, and one with the L.A. boyfriend. They are pictures from past lives that have no bearing on this one at all. I might as well have my wedding album on display.

I never touch anything of Melinda's. I just stand in her space feeling like an intruder.

When I get out of class, I drive to Ben's. He lives on the second floor of a ten-unit, slum apartment building. From what I can tell, only men live here, though sometimes a woman visits and there'll be a fight in the parking lot. If it disrupts whatever Ben's doing, he'll hang his head out the window and yell at the couple, or offer advice.

He opens the door and I hand him a twelve-pack. "I'm making you meatballs," he says.

I follow him into the kitchen and sit on the counter, but the space is too small and I'm just getting in his way. He reaches behind me for the bread crumbs, shakes them into a bowl. He never measures anything.

"I called my ex-husband earlier and he told me that our best friend drank himself to death." He stops what he's doing. "I haven't seen him since I left Meridian but we were really close." I'm upset about it, but mostly I want someone to be upset for me. It's tragic—a tragedy. Or perhaps I just want an excuse to get drunk.

He puts his forearm on my leg because his hands are coated in ground beef and egg, and looks at me too seriously.

"I'm fine—I just hate that he didn't tell me. I have to call his mom. I used to work with her at Curves for Women."

"You worked at Curves for Women?"

"It was basically a sales job and I was terrible at it. I didn't know why anyone would want to join. And it was right next to Papa John's so you had to smell pizza the whole time you're working out." I recall the unpleasantness of measuring the older women: my hands touching their inner thighs and breasts, their bodies warm and slightly damp.

I take a beer from the box and sit at his card table, which holds his laptop and a bunch of precariously stacked papers. When he turns on the fan and the window is open, they fly everywhere. I log onto Facebook and of course my cousin has written me, but as soon as I respond he'll write me back and I'll be in the same boat. It's an ongoing nuisance, this pressure to engage in tedious conversations about dating and work when all I want to do is watch animal videos and stalk my exes. I consider the items in my Amazon cart, wonder if I still want them.

"I got you some of those chips you like," he says, tossing me a bag of Gardetto's.

"I love you." I open it and pick out the crunchy brown pieces, eyeing his bottle of Klonopin. Sometimes he pours the pills into his hand and counts how many are left, and we discuss whether the doctor will believe he lost them or someone stole them and how clichéd that is.

A bottle cap hits the counter; he's already on his second beer. Twelve is not going to be nearly enough.

"It smells so good," I say. Whenever he makes meatballs, I eat them. I don't think about cows or blood or Melinda. "I'm glad you're cooking. I don't have any food at home and I don't go to the grocery store on Friday because it's a madhouse."

"It's a madhouse!" he says, shaking his fist in the air. "A madhouse!"

"What are you talking about?"

"You've never seen *Planet of the Apes*?"

"No."

He shakes his head. "I'm horrified to think how many *Planet of the Apes* references you've missed in your lifetime."

After we've consumed huge plates of meatballs and spaghetti, along with all of the beer and a couple of Jack and Diet Cokes, we get into his bed.

"I'm full as a tick," I say, running a hand over my body, trying to feel my hip bones and ribs; I should start weighing myself, keep a check on things. He rests a hand on my stomach and I wonder if he's imagining a baby, if he wants to impregnate me so we'll be stuck together forever, but then he gets up and stumbles into the bathroom. I run my fingers through my hair, untangling knots while he vomits.

"The last time I threw up it was pink from red wine," I say, as he's brushing his teeth. "It was kind of pretty."

"I threw up pink one time from sweet and sour chicken, but it wasn't pretty. It was chunky and it tasted bad."

We adjust our pillows and watch *Intervention* on his laptop, the woman addicted to pills and bingo. Her husband is about to leave her and she has a lonely, closet-hiding kid. When she's passed out on the floor in broken glass and casserole, Ben says he feels a little better. Then he says, "Seriously, though," as if it's a conversation we've been having all night, "what percent chance do I have?"

We've been over this so many times, it's just a game we play: what is the chance that I'll be with him, that our relationship will ever be more than a friendship stretched to its breaking point?

I think about it and say, "Thirty-seven percent."

"In baseball if you hit the ball thirty-seven percent of the time it's pretty good."

"If you have a thirty-seven percent chance of living it's bad."

"If you have a thirty-seven percent chance of winning the lottery," he counters, "it would be fucking excellent."

"I can't argue with that."

"I've always been lucky," he says, which isn't true.

We watch another episode of *Intervention*, a heroin-addicted prostitute. I've seen this one twice already—it's one of my favorites because the girl is so beautiful. She paints her face in bright colors, twists sections of her hair around a curling iron. Her boyfriend shoots the heroin straight into her jugular.

Ben falls asleep and then jerks himself awake.

"Do you want some water? Can I get you anything?" I ask.

"No," he says. "I'm okay."

I lie in the crook of his arm and say soothing things and it is eleventh grade all over again and I'm in love with a boy who carves things into his arms with the sharp edges of beer cans. I rub Neosporin on his cuts, brush his hair. I hide with him in bedrooms at parties, behind bushes—the world slows, stops. But everything that happened between us could easily be counted in minutes.

In the morning, Ben wants to make me breakfast, but all I want to do is go home and get in my own bed. Once I get there, though, I'm not tired. Melinda is gone, her open doors inviting me in.

I walk into her bedroom—messier than yesterday, panties and wet towels on the floor. I go into her bathroom, which is filled with tiny things: size 5 flip-flops, hotel bottles of lotion, lip gloss you could attach to a key ring. Even her bar of soap is small. Her toilet doesn't look clean, but I pee anyhow and then go back to my room to search for a poem Ben wrote for me. It hung on the refrigerator at my old apartment, but when I moved I folded it up and stuck it in whatever book I was reading and now I can't find it. The poem was about how he was going to turn all of the blackbirds in his heart to flames, or was he going to turn the flames to blackbirds? I look through dozens of books before giving up. It was pretty good but not his best. I'll tell him I misplaced it and he'll make me another copy, write it out on fat-lined paper.

I sit on the counter eating cashews as I gaze out the window, stare at a corner of the blue-tarp roof. I wonder where Melinda has gone, how it's possible that she is so much busier than I am.

Lifting the window, I dislodge the bottle and climb out. I haven't been on a roof since I was a teenager watching a meteor shower at Leslie Hodo's spend-the-night party—ninth grade, tenth? Or maybe I was somewhere else in the house while the others were on the roof; the memory's unclear. It is soft under my feet. I move slowly and bent over, as if this might make the burden of my weight less, and then stand straight to observe our yard and the crack house from this new perspective—the same but different.

Three of the crackheads are already in the garage, two men and one woman, and I'm pretty sure they're looking directly at me but I feel invisible, like I'm so high up no one can see me. No one can touch me. If I crashed through, I would fall into the living room of the man and his dead lover's son. They would come running from different parts of the house and stand over me in their boxer shorts, eager to see what new tragedy had befallen them.

PROPER ORDER

I t is a great big old beautiful house and he stands in my kitchen and says, "This is exactly where I pictured you living," and I take this to mean he thinks I am beautiful, that I am the type of person who should be living in a grand house. I want to see myself as he sees me, as someone who deserves to live here.

He is my student. I am his professor. The house I live in is not mine. It belonged to a famous writer who donated it to the university at which I am employed for one academic year. The house is gated, situated on ninety rolling acres. My friend Clarke says it's the site of an old Cherokee Indian burial ground; a man who wants to sleep with me says that Geeshie Wiley haunts these woods. He sends me links to her songs, asks if he can come out and take a look around. My dog and I have walked every inch of this property, I tell him, though of course this can't be true. We have looked for bones and gravestones, men camping in our woods, but mostly I keep my head empty and walk fast to burn calories; when

my dog jumps up to lick my hand, I imagine her present-
ing me with a skull, her teeth in its eye sockets, a hand in
my hand. And then the police will yellow-tape the place and
the university people will have to move me into a cozy little
condo somewhere off the Square, where the past writers-in-
residence have lived.

There are two ponds, a tennis court, a lumpy croquet
court, and an overgrown baseball field. There is an old home
site, steps leading to nowhere that someone roped off with
vines. There are two garages. In one of them, I found the
famous writer's baseball cards scattered all over the floor and
a neat stack of postcards, the paper cheaply curled. The photograph on the postcard must have been taken there: bare
wooden slats behind him, blue jean shirt, staring directly into
the camera. He was younger then, and newly famous. The
watch on his wrist sits oddly high on his arm. His wedding
band seems to be sliding off his finger.

The famous writer and his wife are everywhere: their
names carved into the driveway, wallpaper they picked out
themselves. His books on the shelf, unsigned, worthless. They
aren't dead but they're gone, which is a little bit like being
dead, and which is, perhaps, the reason I keep moving. This
has been my life for so long now: counting the number of
paychecks until the paychecks run out and I have to find new
paychecks, new boyfriends and friends and living arrange-
ments. There is so much promise in these new places that I
can almost convince myself I'll be different there.

I looked up the baseball cards on eBay and found they
weren't worth much so I gave them to the chair of the English

department to mail back to him. Perhaps it might mean something, my gesture of goodwill.

My students roam about, taking pictures to send to their mothers and aunts, the women who buy his books and have made him so rich he can afford to donate his house and land to the university. They take pictures of the staircase, the carpets. They take pictures out the windows.

"I scare you," I say to the boy. His skin turns red and splotchy. It is remarkable, his skin, a defect, but so pretty. I like people whose insecurities are obvious, when I don't have to pull them out of them.

"I'm not scared of anything," he says, taking a slug of his beer. He's from one of the O states—Ohio or Oklahoma—either way, it means nothing to me. Earlier he touched the side of the house and talked about the grain of wood. He has come here for graduate school and seems to have no idea how he got to this place or why; he wears blazers and collared shirts as if he might learn by dressing the part but it only makes him stand out more.

I imagine unbuttoning his too-tight pants, taking him upstairs to my bedroom. The other students listening as they eat slices of pizza. They say on your deathbed you only regret the things you didn't do and I remember a time when this was the case, when I could picture myself alone in a hospital room and there was nothing I would take back, nothing I would do differently.

The boy is unfailingly late to every class, and every time, he is sorry. During break, he has to run to Starbucks for coffee and sometimes there's a long line—totally out of his control. There are other issues as well: he talks too much; he has a lot of opinions and I almost never agree with any of them but I nod and make neutral-sounding noises while admiring the way he has styled his hair, his nose. And his skin, I love his skin, how it betrays him. I play mediator between him and the other person in class—a very pretty but emaciated young woman who constantly talks about food—who also has strong opinions, and marvel over the fact that they can be so passionate, because I, too, believe I am right, that everyone who disagrees with me is wrong.

It hasn't been long since I was a graduate student, and I don't know how to be anyone's teacher. In an undergraduate psychology course—so many years ago now—my favorite professor said he didn't think of himself as a professor; he considered his own professors the real professors and they must have thought of theirs as the real professors and so no one was ever truly *real*. We're all just derivatives, he said, pretending. He had married one of his students. Businessmen marry their secretaries and professors marry their students. But I am a woman and I won't marry this boy; I might have sex with him, but I won't marry him. I like to think I have some say in the matter.

I hate this house, I think, as I stand in the kitchen with its two dishwashers and double oven, the Sub-Zero refrigerator. There are so many cabinets that I often open three or four before I find what I'm looking for. I imagine lying under the canopy of a magnolia tree until someone comes to scoop me up, but I could lie there for days and no one would come. Perhaps on the fifth day my mother would have gotten worried enough to call the university. She once had the police do a welfare check on my sister in Nashville; two officers came to her door and she'd had to explain, after which she was horrified and refused to speak to our mother for weeks, and so our mother is less inclined to react.

I'm supposed to be working on my second novel but I can't write because there's all this time and space and no one watching, no one checking in; only one day a week that I have to show up to teach. I don't even know if I want to be a writer anymore. I've become so self-conscious of what I'm writing and why, and whether I ever had any talent in the first place. My sister—who left the music business for a job in nursing—says that nearly every band's first album is their best because they're working in a vacuum; there's no outside pressure to *be* something or to do something great. And so I spend the majority of my time watching cable, which I haven't had in years. I watch the ID Channel and consider becoming a detective, or committing a murder. I think I could do either sufficiently well at this point. I only watch it during the day because if I fall asleep when it's on the stories seep into my dreams: people missing, rape, women buried alive with their hands bound as if in prayer.

Other days I stand on the porch and think: *I love it here. I love this house. I love the birds. I love the geese and the ponds and the hills and the tennis court and the woods and I love that this is "my land," if only for a little while.* I sing and run and my dog jumps up to lick my hand, offering me nothing more than a stick, and we pretend we're in a musical. These are the best days, but still I do not write.

I observe one of my students going into the bathroom for the third time and stop myself from saying something. He once left his pipe on the floor of my office and I brought it to class and handed it to him in front of several other students. This man is writing a memoir about his time in the TSA and fears he's on a government watchlist, which makes me like him best (besides the boy, but I don't really like him, not really).

The boy tells me he has relatives in Savannah he sees on holidays. I look at the bowls of nuts and pretzels that I've positioned around the kitchen. "Savannah has the most amazing St. Paddy's Day Parade," he says, "one of the best in the world." He has ties to the South, he wants me to know, having already learned that women down here don't date men they can't trace. Not me, but others.

"Maybe you could come with me?" he says, and I want to grab his arm. God, his arm. It's like a thigh. "That might be inappropriate. I'm sorry."

"You won't be my student in a month." And then, because I think the others might be picking up on something, I ask him loudly if he plays tennis. I say, "Y'all are welcome to use the court anytime. No one ever uses it."

"I can learn," he says.

I climb onto the island to screw in one of the lightbulbs; it comes back to life. I look down at my students eating pizza and drinking Coke—most of them don't drink alcohol—and wish I could stay there, stretch my body across its length while they glance nervously at each other and giggle. I open another beer and excuse myself to the bathroom where I text my boyfriend, the doctor. All of my exes have been reduced to two words, three at most, and this one, though still current, still in play, I think of as The Doctor. The famous writer is also a doctor. My sister says this doctor only wants to sleep in the famous doctor's bed—it must be his dream—but all of the mattresses are new, as is most of the furniture, and my boyfriend prefers for me to sleep at his house. The only person who really likes it here is my mother. She comes to get away from my father. She brings her little dog and we go on exploring missions in which the dogs peer into holes and run through fields of tall grass. Once I let them swim in the pond and laughed as they struggled to keep their heads above water. Another time the little dog fell into a hole and I had to climb in to get her out.

I'm watching *Bob's Burgers*, he texts back. How are things going with your students? I don't reply. I feel my lower body, swelled with blood, and hope my period starts soon.

Once, after he came inside me, I said, "Let's have a baby." I can't explain these things to myself. Do I say them because I want him to break up with me or do I say them because it's what I truly want, deep down in some unknowable part of myself? I have never wanted a child, but perhaps this is because I've never been with anyone who wanted a child with me. He was kind about it. He said that we should do things in the proper order. But since my divorce, eight years ago, there is no order, proper or otherwise. I think I love someone and they love me and then something comes along and ruins it. They let me believe that I am that something.

In the dining room, I find a few of my students flipping

through some old university annuals—1904, 1906—beautifully bound in soft leather. The fraternities used to publish them, their clubs interspersed with poems and drawings of farm animals, profiles of women with pinned-up hair. I got an email recently from the secretary who was looking for a particular yearbook, and then someone from the foundation contacted me about it, and then someone else. I thought it might be rare, the only copy, but I saw the secretary at brunch and she told me they wanted to destroy that year because one of the fraternities had formed a KKK club, had dressed up in white robes with cutout eyes, and the university wanted it gone.

We walk the rooms. The house really *is* beautiful. There are windows everywhere and a table for twelve, high ceilings, chandeliers. When I first moved in, I imagined the house full of people and laughter, just like this, footsteps going up and down the stairs, doors opening and closing. But it hasn't been like this; it hasn't been anything like this. I am alone, far enough from town that it's considered the country, though it's not that far from town and is not the country.

The boy follows me around, asks questions. He wants to know what it's like to live here. They all want to know what it's like.

Nights, I climb out onto the roof with its not-too-steep incline to smoke a bowl; the window opens easily—all I have to do is throw a leg out. We stand in front of this window and I open it. This is what I want to show them: here is where I sit nights. When you think of me, imagine me here. But I don't actually sit out here very often. Only after I've had too much to drink, when the potential for hurting myself is greatest.

They peer into my bedroom, admire the size of my bathtub, the separate shower and all of the closet space.

The boy comes up behind me and I ask how old he is, though I know how old he is. The only correct answer is that he is old enough and I am young enough. And I'm old enough to know better but not so old to take myself seriously when I talk about the young people today with their pretentions and noise music and carefully crafted carelessness. Their highly developed sensitivities to sexism (but not so much to racism or classism because it is still the Deep South). *Stop policing my body,* I once overhead a female student say to a male—not mine—and I smiled at her, thinking the comment ironic.

As we stand awkwardly around my bedroom, I tell them things happen in the house that I can't explain. There are noises. Lights come on. Garage doors open by themselves and books are moved. It's an old house and there are rational explanations for all of these things, or at least most of them. The country is noisy as shit and nails don't hold and wiring is faulty and I drink a lot so I can't say whether or not I closed a door or moved a book, at least not for certain.

The women ask about an alarm system—nonexistent. I tell them that my dog would happily lick the feet of an intruder, though I don't know if this is true, and that dozens if not hundreds of people know the gate code: the year the university began. I say this with pride: I am okay here; I'm tough. But on my worst nights, I don't sleep. I lock my bedroom door and lie awake planning escape routes. I imagine myself climbing out of the bathroom window, shimmying and jumping my way down without a scratch. I am unbelievably limber in these imaginings and there is a part of me that wants to be tested. But the facts show that I am bad in an emergency, that I will stand in one spot and scream until rescued, which is why my father refuses to give me a gun.

And then we gather in the living room where they take turns reading their stories. I have given them guidelines: the stories must be under 750 words; they must be in first person and they must have been written this semester. They don't follow them. As graduate students, they know they don't have to.

The boy reads a highly sexualized piece that isn't shocking so much as it is awkward and I wonder if he's chosen this particular piece for me. I look at the carpet as if I'm concentrating very hard and think about my own early writing, how I wrote things that shouldn't have been written and how it had taken me years to figure out the difference between writing the truth and writing something explicit and ugly that only looked like the truth. But these things are so hard to explain. Often, in class, I find myself talking about the mystery of writing. I find myself relying on *rules*, which I never thought I'd have to rely on. Write and read: these are the only rules, but they are unhappy when you tell them this; it's too difficult and they don't really like reading all that much. And half the class writes about mermaids and aliens and strange apocalyptic worlds, which are all so similar, and I wonder what the hell any of us are doing. How I could possibly teach anyone anything.

It goes on and on. Deirdre and the emaciated girl and the Chinese guy and my TSA friend and their stories must be seven, eight pages long. Every time someone begins to read I try to determine how many pages they're working with, the thickness of the stack.

When it's finally over, I've had nothing to eat and five or six beers.

I send the students home with leftover pizza. I even bag up the nuts and pretzels. While I say goodbye to everyone, the boy stays in the bathroom and then emerges, the light behind him, smiling triumphantly. His skin perfectly normal.

"I thought you carpooled."

"I drove myself," he says.

There are only a couple of beers left so I make him drive me to the gas station where it is embarrassing how well they know me. They know what I eat and drink and give me coupons, their cards, because it's a college town and they are trying to improve themselves. I wonder if they think of me when men come into the store late at night to buy condoms, though I haven't sent anyone over in a month, at least.

"It's gotten weirdly foggy out," I say to the girl, and she says she's glad she's inside because it's spooky as hell out, and then she goes into a story about how she saw an owl for the first time in her life, how it turned its whole neck around to look at her.

"Owls are predators. They could take off with a small dog, easy." I glance at her name tag, tell myself to remember it this time.

"You be careful out there," she says.

Back at the house, the boy and I sit on the porch. It's the end of October but it's still warm and bullfroggy. My dog licks my leg and I want to pick her up and carry her upstairs to my bedroom where she'd be uncomfortable but I'd shut her in and make her stay with me anyway. She doesn't like stairs. Occasionally, I carry her up them, though she's thirty pounds and acts like I'm torturing her the whole time.

"What's wrong with her eye?" the boy asks.

"Nothing. She's an Australian shepherd mix."

"Is she blind?"

"No—she can see just fine."

The bottom half of her left eye is blue-gray and craggy; it looks like a mountain range. This is what I tell him. He doesn't say anything. "Can't you see it? Can't you see the mountain in her eye?" I want to touch his leg, most of all, which is so thick with muscle it is nearly fat. I want to grab his arm, so near me I could rub my own against it. I've heard he's in love with another of my students, a talented girl from Georgia with very short hair. She told me she writes at least 1,500 words a day, every day, which depressed me. I hate to hear how hard people are working.

"Why are you still here?" I ask, but this only makes him ask if he should leave and that's not what I was getting at; it's also the only response to my question. Soon he will be with this other girl, this young girl he loves, and they'll get engaged and live in a small apartment where they'll write their stories and drink their Starbucks, dream their big dreams. They will do things in the proper order and they'll be happy. I can see it all so clearly. Don't mess it up, I want to tell him. Don't fuck things up because once you start fucking up it's so hard to stop and there comes a point at which you simply don't know how to do anything else anymore.

AT ONE TIME THIS WAS THE
LONGEST COVERED WALKWAY
IN THE WORLD

"I'm dead," the boy says.

"You're not dead," his father says.

"I'm dead," the boy insists, draping his body over the arm of his chair. The people at the next table look at him, at me, and smile.

"Don't be weird, son," his father says, opening the boy's shark book. "Look at this one—what kind is this?"

The boy looks at it. "Hammerhead," he says. His father turns the pages, and he says: "cow shark, prickly shark, zebra." He takes a swig of his root beer, which is in a brown bottle like our beers.

"Did you know that you shouldn't wear a watch or other shiny things in the ocean?" I ask the boy. "A shark will think you're a fish and try to eat you." He shakes his head. "It's the glint," I say, "like fish scales," tipping my bare wrist back and forth, but he doesn't know what a glint is. He's only four.

I look at his father, my boyfriend, who is texting someone, probably his ex-wife.

The boy's burger comes and his father cuts it in half and the boy takes a bite out of one half and puts it down and then picks up the other half and takes a bite. My boyfriend waves the waitress over and asks for ketchup. I order another beer. There is something wrong with my stomach, an ulcer maybe, and I know I shouldn't be drinking but I seem to be incapable of living the kind of life where I eat nutritious meals and exercise and go to bed at a decent hour, or I can only live like this for a short period of time before fucking it all up again.

Flies circle the boy's burger. One lands on the edge of the basket and makes its way along the rim. The boy and I watch it while my boyfriend stares at his phone. The fly moves so fast I can't see its individual legs and then it stops abruptly and crosses one leg over another and scrubs them together. I wave my hand around. My boyfriend sets his phone down and unfolds a napkin, lays it over his son's food.

It is August, too hot to be sitting outside. I look at the kid, who would never pass for mine, and hate him a little. He has a white scar that snakes up the middle finger of his left hand (from a skateboarding accident when he was two, he tells me), blond hair, and brown eyes. My boyfriend's eyes are blue. I want to ask my boyfriend what color his ex-wife's eyes are because if they're blue then the boy isn't his and we could be spending our nights alone.

On Saturday afternoon, I go over to my boyfriend's house to swim. He lives with his mother because his ex-wife got the house and everything in it. He talks about his circumstances constantly—the things he used to have, how he owned his own home at twenty, how badly he wants to get out of this town but can't.

He and his wife grew apart, he says, which could mean anything, but more than likely it means she found him intolerable or fell in love with someone else.

On the kitchen counter, there's a paper bag containing beer and vodka and mixers and I know I won't be going home tonight, that I'll end up staying in the guest bedroom, wishing his body was pressed against mine. And in the morning, I'll wake up and tiptoe into the room where he and his son will be passed out on top of the covers with their hands in their pants. I like the idea of the boy, how much a father can love his son, but I don't like the actual son, who is screaming because he can't find his swim trunks.

"Where did you last see them?" I ask, bending down so I'm eye level, my voice high and false. I don't even speak this way to dogs.

"Would you grab him a Capri Sun?" my boyfriend says to me. "Let's put on Jamie's," he says to the boy, leading him into the other room with a hand on his back.

I pluck the tiny straw off, unwrap it and poke the uneven side into the pouch as indicated, while my boyfriend helps the boy into his cousin's swim trunks. Then he comes back into the kitchen to mix two vodka and tonics and the three of us go outside.

They do backflips off the diving board and swim butterfly as I paddle back and forth, avoiding their wake, because I

have my contacts in, because they remind me I'm a girl. I
wonder how my boyfriend would act with a daughter, if he'd
teach her to change a flat tire and skateboard and play soccer,
or if he'd love her less because he'd failed to teach her to do
these things. One time my father tried to teach me to drive a
stick shift; for weeks after, I practiced in my sleep.

My boyfriend wraps his limbs around one of the wooden
beams that holds up the porch, shimmies up it in increments
like a bug, and climbs onto the roof. The roof is flat. I could
see myself up there: looking at the stars, smoking a joint. He
jogs to the other end and then turns and runs, launching himself into the middle of the pool.

He swims beneath me, raking his fingers down my body
as he goes.

Later, the three of us are in bed, watching men surf the
biggest waves in the world from his laptop. When the waves
break, the men get lost in the white foaminess and Jet Skis
rush out to search for them.

"Is she going home?" the boy asks. "I think she should go
home now."

"She's staying here tonight," he says, an arm around each
of us. I'm not uncomfortable with the situation, but then I
think about it and decide that I *should* be uncomfortable and
then I am.

"Come tuck me in," I say, yanking on my boyfriend's arm.
He follows me back to the guest bedroom and turns the fan
on, stands there while I take off my shorts and move all the
pillows to one side and get under the covers. He sits beside

me, pulls the sheet up to my neck like my mother used to do. Then he kisses my forehead and closes the door behind him.

My boyfriend has his son every other night. Every other night, I don't see him, or I see him and the boy, or I feel guilty because he has passed the boy off on his mother. This afternoon, he has passed the boy off. He comes over to my house and stands on his head and falls and then stands on his head and falls again and I picture the guy who lives below me looking at his ceiling, waiting for the next thud. "Let's go kick the soccer ball," he says, jumping up. I don't know how to play soccer, though I used to watch my ex-husband play. I'd hand him bananas for leg cramps, cold bottles of water.

He skateboards on the sidewalk while I follow, his soccer ball under my arm like an athlete, circling back so I won't get too far behind. Talking the whole time. His energy makes me nervous and dull, like I have nothing to say that might interest him, like I won't be able to hold his attention for long. When he's like this, I find myself unable to locate words, lose my train of thought. I jog to keep up and the cars don't honk like they do when I'm just a white girl in a dress walking alone. He leads me to the train station. It is one of the things I like most, how he doesn't force me into the position of having to admit I don't know what I want.

"At one time this was the longest covered walkway in the world," he says, and I lie on his skateboard, which is actually a longboard, a type I've never seen, and he pushes me down the covered walkway. I turn my head to look at the rusted train cars and a series of low, redbrick buildings, the puffy clouds splotched with dark spots. The sun disappears behind one of them and the world goes dim and I'm reminded that the ugly derelict things only make the world more beautiful. I put my feet on the concrete to stop myself, and he bends down and kisses me. I touch his face, slick with sweat.

He pulls a bandanna from his pocket and offers it to me first. Then we kick the soccer ball back and forth. I try to kick it up into my hands like he does, but I miss until he says, "Like that, but put your hands out." *It's like magic. Like keep your eye on the ball.*

He does a backflip, lands on his feet. "You should do that in the grass," I say, as a bus pulls up. No one gets on or off. The driver stares straight ahead and keeps his hands on the wheel.

"Come on," he says, skating while I dribble. "Don't let it get too far ahead of you," he says, "stay in control of it." Cars fly by. I look at the people inside, more grotesque than the ones walking around in the world, turning their heads to look at us. I wonder if they just pick up fried chicken and drive back home, if they ever go anywhere besides Walmart. I kick the ball into the street and he skates out to retrieve it, kicks it to me. We're like a gang, the two of us, and the kid tucked safely away at his mother's so we can recall the cute things he said about how babies are made and life after death and smile.

I follow him to a park, a small grassy area and a fountain. The last time we were here, we saw a couple with a picnic basket being photographed in the dark. He reminds me of this. I remind him how he slipped and fell on his back so perfectly I thought he'd done it on purpose.

We walk over to the fountain, which is surrounded by concrete benches, spaced in such a way that you shouldn't jump from one to the other of them, but he does, and then I stand on one and look at the next one and he says, "You can do it." He holds out his hand and I swat at it and jump, and then jump another, following him around the fountain feeling drunk and careless, like if I hurt myself it will be his fault, which makes hurting myself seem okay, necessary even. And then we stop and take off our shoes and cover up as many water holes as we can with our feet and hands.

I shower while he goes outside to smoke. He comes back and smashes his forehead to the frosted glass, his hands cupping either side of his face. I pretend not to see him and then I look at him, surprised, and turn the water off.

He hands me a bundle of tiny weed-like flowers so small they can't be put in water; they would float like tea leaves.

"You make me so happy," I say.

"That makes me happy," he says, digging the pads of his fingers into my scalp. My hair drips onto the mat.

"How come?"

He shrugs and says, "I'm going to take a quick shower and then let's go out." He loves going to bars, drinking and stepping into hair-trigger conversations that could easily deteriorate into fights. He won't admit this, though—he says it's his face, that it attracts fists.

While we wait for our sushi, we sit at the bar and drink, draw on napkins with tiny pencils. I write: I ♥ Richie. He draws a picture of a dinosaur, smoking and taking a shit. The caption above it says *Dinos died from Sneezys.*

"What's a sneezy?"

"It's a blunt," he says, "or a whore who won't leave you alone."

"That's like every entry in the Urban Dictionary."

I push my napkin in front of him and tell him I love him. He doesn't say anything and then he says he can't say it back. If I'd thought there'd been a chance of it, I wouldn't have mentioned it.

"How do you know you love me?" he asks.

"I don't know—because sometimes it's all I can think. Sometimes it's the only thing that'll stay in my head."

He considers this and says, "It doesn't mean I don't love you. It only means I can't say it." And then he gives me some reasons but I don't listen. Probably he is saying love is terrifying and financially ruinous and stuff like that. I scratch out *I ♥ Richie* and flip the napkin over. I draw more hearts, dozens of them, in all sizes, that grow closer and closer together until there's no more room. Then I pencil them in. I've always doodled hearts; it has nothing to do with anything.

I think about the things he does for me—how he insists on paying and pulls out chairs, how he walks on the outside of the street when there's no sidewalk so he'll be the one that gets hit, and wonder why these things don't matter more—they are actual things, whereas the other is just a group of words I've said to a bunch of people who are no longer around, people I don't even think about.

On the way back to my house, he stops at the gas station.

He likes the make-your-own-six-packs, always gets two of each so we can drink the same thing at the same time.

He opens a couple of Fat Tires and we sit on my floor and look at his pictures from India on his laptop: he's in a rickshaw, a hookah bar, a train station. He took a picture of his feet from every bed he slept in. There are pictures of him with other mustached men who called him brother. Somewhere, in a camera belonging to a girl from Arkansas, there's a picture of him holding a dead baby he plucked out of the Ganges; he thought it was a pile of rags. "We weren't supposed to take pictures on the Ganges," he says, "fucking bitch." He tells me how the girl from Arkansas kept trying to have sex with him. Except for his ex-wife, all of his stories involving women sound like this: the girl wanted to fuck him, and he did, or didn't, and either way she was angry. He lost jobs, friends, places to live.

When the slideshow is over, he shows me a picture of him and his ex-wife dressed as Adam and Eve for Halloween. His hair is disheveled; he's holding an apple and looking away from the camera. Her face looks kind of like a boy's, but she has long hair and skinny legs and large breasts. They are possibly the most beautiful couple I have ever seen.

Today, a postcard arrives while I'm eating cheese toast he made in the oven, watching him walk around with his shirt off. It's from a man named Frank, an older gay man he knew in Tallahassee. He would come home from work and find Frank passed out on his patio furniture. Now, Frank writes him letters, dozens of them that go unopened. I read the card to myself and then read it aloud: German friends, a tourist trap, an island. It is like a regular postcard in that it says nothing.

"I hate it when he calls them his German friends like I don't know them," he says.

I put the postcard on the stack, wondering if there are any checks inside the envelopes and if he'd be willing to cash them. Then I pick up an empty box of Diet Dr Pepper. "I thought you didn't drink this stuff," I say, turning it upside down.

"It's a mask," he says. He shows me the two, lopsided eyeholes. His room is full of helmets and trucks and plastic men with movable parts. Once, he sent me a picture of himself wearing a chest plate, holding a sword and shield: *Did anyone order a knight in shining armor?* I watch him undress behind his open door, and glance at his mother in the kitchen, painting watercolors. I wonder what she thinks of me, if she wonders what I'm doing here. I go to the bathroom and put my swimsuit on. The bathroom is decorated in sailboats—on the shower curtain and bath mat, hanging above the toilet—though we are nowhere near the ocean.

I open the sliding glass door, where the dogs lick my hands, and take a towel from a chairback. My boyfriend comes out and picks up his clippers, tends his marijuana plant. His mother doesn't know it's a marijuana plant; when she had a party last week for the diabetes children, he had to relocate it.

"Come smell," he says.

I lean into the hairy little pods, say it smells good, and

then go lie down. I think about his ex-wife in a flesh-colored suit, leaves covering her nipples and vagina, and try to read but there are the dogs and the sun and my boyfriend, who is shirtless, who likes to climb things and fling himself off.

"I'm your cabana boy," he says, bringing me a beer. "Pale Ale okay?"

"Yes, thanks."

"Don't be too polite to the cabana boy," he says. "Cabana boys should be treated like shit." He tells me all I have to do when I want another is to hold up my empty bottle and waggle it. I try it out and he says, "Yes, good, like that," and goes back to pruning his plant. Then he chases the leaves and pine straw out of the pool with a net while I squeeze my breasts together, arrange my body into what I hope are alluring shapes. He doesn't notice. After a while, I go to the bathroom to check my face and hair and body in the mirror. I lean into it and wonder if he can see me, why he doesn't see me.

When I come back out, his ex-wife is there, their kid. She's not as pretty in person, moving around.

She looks at me and says, "Hey, Alice," and I look at the pool, the blue water rippling. I didn't know she knew my name. Of course she knows my name, but I didn't figure she'd have the balls to say it. I wrap a towel around my shoulders and sit at the table, pick up an empty bottle and set it back down. She hands my boyfriend the boy's bag, a tote that says EGGS MILK BREAD BOOKS and they stand close together and talk in quiet voices. *Just get back together,* I think. *Just admit you still love each other and it'll be a whole lot easier on all of us.*

The boy walks over to me with a dinosaur in each hand.

"Which one looks the scariest?" he asks. They are the same size with white, pointy teeth. He presses a button on the red one's tail and it makes a pitiful roar.

"Does the other one make noise?" I ask.

"They all make noise." He hands me the red one and presses the blue one's button; it makes a slightly different pitiful roar.

"Not that authentic, really."

"Which one is the scariest?" he asks.

"This one," I say, indicating the one I'm holding. I open its jaw and stick my finger down its throat, make a puke sound.

After she leaves, my boyfriend sits next to me and squeezes my leg just above the knee. "This is how the horse eats the apple," he says, which is something we say to each other, something we do.

I meet my boyfriend and his son for happy hour. Dinner, we call it, when it's the three of us. Tonight the boy brings along an enormous book of every bird that ever existed. You press a button to hear the call of a cardinal, an eastern brown pelican, a mockingbird. I turn the pages and drink vodka and cranberries, two for one. We read about the dodo and how its extinction was due to a combination of its inability to fly and its fearlessness of humans. This seems profound: a large, unwieldy bird that couldn't fly, a species that developed in isolation so it never learned to fear.

After ordering his son's food, Richie goes inside to take a shot at the bar, or to use the bathroom—he doesn't say—and I continue looking at birds with the boy, flipping the pages without interest now that he is gone.

"There's an owl at my house," the boy says, digging a matchbox van from his pocket. "My mom's house." He sets the Volkswagen on the table and looks up at me and I poke him in the stomach. He looks confused and then pokes me back, a little too low. I press a button and we hear the call of the great horned owl. He shows me the inside of the van, how there is a table and a sink, how it is just like a real one.

My boyfriend sends me a text: I met someone who knows you.

How interesting, I text back, sure it's a girl, probably the hottest girl I know, begging to suck him off. Twenty minutes later, he comes back out, pays the bill and collects his son.

After he takes the boy home and puts him to bed, he comes over and crawls into bed with me.

"It was a guy named Darren," he says. Darren tried to convince him that he believed in God, that all of his good deeds, which mostly involve helping stranded motorists, are based on his desire to get into heaven.

I went home with Darren one night from a bar.

"How do you know that guy again?" he asks, as if we've been over this before.

"I met him at 206."

"He acted like he knew you pretty well."

"He doesn't. That was before you."

"Yeah, but the guy is insane," he says. "He's crazy."

After Darren and I slept together, he told me he was psychic. I was drunk and all I could think to ask was when I would die, if he could tell me when I'd die. He had no information.

"I can't relax," I say. "I can never fully relax with you." *When you leave me, you won't really be leaving me,* I think, *you'll be leaving the girl you thought I was, who was kind of like me, but not.* He presses his lips to my forehead for a long time like boys do when they love you or want to convince you they love you so you'll have sex with them.

"What can I do?" he asks, and I tell him he's already doing everything, which is true. He calls me all the time and brings me gifts, drives across town to see me every day; it is more than anyone else has ever done. We kiss for a while. When we kiss, I don't think about how it is for him, if he's enjoying it—it is possibly the only time I am myself. I flip over and pull his arm around me. Then I push it off and get out of bed and open the window. I like to hear the trains pass through when I'm up at night with my hand on his chest, listening to him breathe and grind his teeth, thinking about what I might do differently in order to keep him.

BIG BAD LOVE

The roller skates are busted and the bikes have flat tires and the wagon is full of leaves and rainwater, but they're used to these things. They pedal harder, skate without bending their knees. They make adjustments. I sit in a chair by the door and sweat. Fat drops race down my sides, cool and itchy as bugs.

Diamond pulls the wagon in front of me and the handle smacks the concrete. I ignore her so she shoves it into my legs and I continue ignoring her so she goes and stands in an ant bed. When she starts screaming, I run over and pick her up, move her to the sidewalk and take off one of her sandals, swipe at the ants while she stomps.

Inside, we sit on the couch under an enormous photograph of the former television star. The photograph is a head shot, black-and-white with a loopy signature at the bottom. The former television star comes at Christmas, brings presents and lets the children touch her arms. She wears her hair in a ponytail so we'll think she's a real person.

I put Diamond's legs in my lap and smear Neosporin on her bites.

"My legs ashy," she says, dipping her fingers into the Neosporin and rubbing.

"Don't do that. I'll get you some lotion."

"Lemme do your hair."

"My hair's already done," I say, though it's only hanging loose, wash and go. I touch the darker spots on her arm, places that haven't healed well.

In my boss's office, I open the supply cabinet, which is full of Dial soap and Suave shampoo, a box of thin plastic combs in primary colors. I take out a comb, red and bendy, and hand it to her. Then I sit in one of the kids' chairs and she sits on the couch and rests her legs on my shoulders. She brushes my hair back roughly with her fingers.

"Use the comb," I say, "and be gentle. I have a sensitive head."

She thinks this is funny, a sensitive head. She runs the comb through to the tips and twists it into a tight bun, announcing it Chinese style before letting go. After she's gotten all the knots out, I tell her we have to check on the baby.

The baby room has five cribs, four of them empty.

The baby is asleep, snoring lightly because her nose is stopped up. Her scalp is loaded with what appears to be dandruff only the Indian doctor said it was fungus. He said in children it's always fungus. Her diaper is so wet I can feel it breaking apart so I pick her up and place her on the changing table. Then I go across the hall to restock the diapers and wet wipes, knowing she won't fall off. She isn't like other babies, who fidget and need to be entertained.

"Don't worry, this fungus thing'll clear up and you'll be good as new. It's probably just psychosomatic." She blinks. She understands me completely. She could be the child savior, the one come to save us all.

When she first got here the back of her head was flat because her fourteen-year-old mother never picked her up. I've been teaching her to roll over; I've been teaching her colors and shapes and the parts of her body.

I shove her dirty diaper into the Genie, which a rich volunteer brought over last week. The woman donated two of them along with a crib, though the extra crib only made the room crowded. The shelter hasn't been at capacity in months. I don't know why. We live in the poorest state in the country; we have an abundance of unemployed people and more illegitimate babies than we know what to do with. There's something going on that I don't know about but no one tells me anything because I established myself early as someone who can't keep a secret.

I place her back in the crib and push a ratty little doll next to her so she won't feel alone, and then Diamond and I go outside to gather pecans in our shirts. We eat the good ones and chuck the bad ones into the street where a funeral procession is in progress, the cars passing slowly with their headlights on. The cars going in the opposite direction stop out of respect and I wonder if people do this in other towns. I wouldn't want to live in a town where people didn't do this.

"Maybe we could go to the pool later," I say.

Diamond screams and tells the other girls and they all scream and I tell them they'll have to ask Miss Monique and be extra nice for the rest of the day.

In the kitchen, Monique is flouring pork chops, an open number 10 can of black-eyed peas next to the stove. Because I have a college degree and I'm not obese, I'm in charge of nutrition, but she insists on frying everything. Even the vegetables have hunks of fat floating in them.

"The food bank didn't come again," she says.

"Oh?" I say. I'm relieved that the food bank didn't come because I'm responsible for going down there and collecting it, piling the boxes onto a cart and pushing the cart up a hill that doesn't usually seem like a hill but becomes a great challenge on food bank days. Sometimes Bruce helps me. Bruce is a young guy they've hired to help Octavio with maintenance but half the time he's leaning against a truck, smoking. The older girls slip him notes. They ask him directly for the things they want: cigarettes, money, sex. It doesn't seem like a strategy that would work but it frequently does.

The girls ask Monique if they can go to the pool and she tells me she can't find the cornmeal. I know it's because there isn't any but I unlock the pantry anyway, the girls trailing behind me, and look around. It's the end of the month and there's hardly more than powdered milk and white-labeled cans of soup. Diamond plucks a half-sucked sucker out of a jar of party toothpicks and sticks it in her mouth. Angel finds an old peanut butter egg and I find a jumbo bag of marshmallows. I squeeze one and it's still soft so I tuck it behind a big box of Bisquick.

"We're out," I say. "Put it on the list and I'll get some next time I'm at Walmart."

Monique curses under her breath, loud enough for me to make out the particulars but not loud enough for me to call her out on it, which I learned the hard way.

We leave her in the kitchen and go from room to room, rummaging through drawers and closets. I find swimsuits for Diamond and Tasia and Brie, but I can't find one for Angel so I sort through bags of donated socks and nightshirts until I locate a stretched-out bikini.

"Rainbow print is really hot right now," I say, tossing it to her.

She takes off her clothes and puts the bottoms on, turns around so I can tie the triangle top. Then she walks up and down the hall with her hard little stomach bulging, modeling it for us.

Right now we only have young girls—Tasia is the oldest at eleven—and they don't hate me like the older ones do. The older girls threaten to beat me up, call the cops, leave this place and never come back. Our policy is to let them go; we watch as they run down the street with whatever they've managed to strap to their backs and then call the police and their social workers. We never see them again. Their names are erased from the whiteboards, their files shelved. It seems incredible, how easily they are forgotten, but this is also our policy: don't talk about the girls who leave; it upsets the others, or encourages them.

I keep waiting for them to return, one by one, dirty and beat-up, or all together, like a group of alien abductees emerging from the fog as if nothing happened.

I sit on the edge and dangle my legs in the water. It's a public pool in a park full of concrete. There are empty flowerpots and bathrooms with metal mirrors like they have at rest stops. The baby is in my arms, making me sweat. I lift her above my head and she laughs so I pretend like I'm eating her hand and she pulls the sunglasses off my face and drops them in the water.

Diamond paddles over with her Dora the Explorer floaties to fetch them. She hands them to me and I wipe the lenses on my shirt while she moves up and down on my foot.

"It's impolite to hump someone's foot," I say, and she shows me her ear as if I misspoke.

In the shallow end, Angel holds Tasia's head under water. They call each other motherfucker and then they're calling each other baldhead and cross-eye and scarface, making motherfucker seem generous. Monique and I look at each other and look away. Sometimes she'll pull them aside and explain hell—how hot it is there, how all the ice cream melts before you can get your lips on it—but today we don't care. I want to lie in the grass under a tree and take a nap but there's only a rectangle of concrete surrounded by basketball courts and parking lots, Monique sitting under the single umbrella reading a romance novel.

"I'm gone take these off," Diamond says, yanking at her floaties.

"You'll have to get out if you take them off."

"I know how to swim."

"I know you do," I say, "I know," though she doesn't know how. They imagine all sorts of lives for themselves other than the ones they're living and I try to let them have them.

When we get back to the cottage, I adjust the temperature control with a butter knife. I put soap and toilet paper in all of the bathrooms and then sit on the couch with the girls to watch *The Little Mermaid*. They are despondent, listless. I ask Tasia what she wants to be when she grows up and she tells me a secretary or a waitress at Outback Steakhouse and I don't give her the speech I usually give them, where I tell them they can be doctors and lawyers and astronauts, where I tell them success has no bounds. I should try to mix it up a bit, anyhow—it's not as if I could be a doctor or a lawyer or an astronaut, either. I took the LSAT but I did it out of a sense of duty, to prove I wouldn't do well on it. There are other things besides doctors and lawyers and astronauts. And how many astronauts even exist in the world? A hundred? Five hundred? Perhaps there are thousands upon thousands of them, all waiting to go up into space.

"Who wants a snack?" I ask, and they perk up.

They follow me into the kitchen. Tasia opens the refrigerator and takes out a brick of government cheese.

"Ask first," I say. There's no door to the kitchen but they're not supposed to cross the invisible line unless given permission. They're not supposed to open the refrigerator or get a cup of water. I think about a border-crossing documentary I watched a few nights ago and how a man claimed he didn't believe in borders, how stupid I thought that was. It didn't matter if you didn't believe in them—other people believed in them.

I pass out graham crackers and plastic tumblers of Kool-Aid and we go outside while Monique feeds the baby. I try pushing three of them at once, but Diamond is angry because I'm not pushing her high enough. She becomes more and more upset until I finally give up and go inside and get a chair, sit by the door with my book.

She throws her body to the ground while I ignore her, and then she comes over and climbs into my lap.

"Why do you have to get so dirty?" I ask, brushing her knees. She twirls a finger around a strand of my hair. I wait for her to yank but she just twirls and twirls and I think about the first time I took her home, parked the van in my driveway and introduced her to my husband. We sat on the couch and ate cold pizza.

"Ooh, that nasty," she says, grabbing the book out of my hand. On the cover, two people are making out in the back-seat of a car. They are thin and young and beautiful and the picture somehow implies that passion requires these things, that the rest of us are going to miss out.

"It's not nasty. They're just kissing."

"You nasty," she says. I kiss her forehead. My boss stands in the doorway and asks if she can see me for a minute.

"Sure," I say, lifting Diamond off my lap. I follow her back to her office, a Styrofoam to-go box open on her desk: fried chicken and mashed potatoes and green beans, a soggy-bottomed roll on top. She eats a wing as she tells me how much money it's costing us to keep Diamond. "Each month, the state gives us less for her care," she says. I look at pictures of her grandson, the framed certificates on the walls. She wants me to start collecting my own certificates—there's a weeklong food service conference next month where I will learn how to weigh and measure, what constitutes a serving of protein. Where I will make friends with cafeteria ladies from all over the state.

"I found her a home where she'll be the only child," she says. "The woman's specially trained to deal with problem children." We both know Diamond isn't the kind of child anyone can be trained for, but I don't say this. She puts a wing down and picks up a thigh.

I find Diamond in her room, sitting on the bed she doesn't sleep in.

"You're leaving," I say. "We have to pack your stuff."

I fold her shirts and dresses while she kicks her toys into a pile. I haven't seen a single suitcase since I've been here. I think about organizing a suitcase drive—people would get behind it. I hand her a garbage bag and she tosses the toys in, each one slamming the floor, while I stack her clothes into the other bag as neatly as possible. When we're finished, I look around the room. The eight rooms in the shelter are identical but decorated with different lamps and bedspreads, different pictures above the beds. I can't imagine anyone else sleeping under her ladybugs.

We sit on her bed and she runs her hand up and down my arm like the black girls do sometimes, imagining what it feels like to have white skin. Nothing special, I tell them—hurts the same, bleeds.

"You pretty," she says, digging her nails into my arm. I don't say anything so she digs harder, her eyes all pupil.

"Thank you."

"No, you ugly."

"That's not nice."

"I'm kidding—you pretty, you pretty," she says.

"Stop." I push her hand away.

Diamond is preoccupied with ugly. She wants to know if she's ugly, if I'm ugly, if the baby full of scars and fungus is ugly. I tell her we are all beautiful. I tell her we are children of God.

"Come on. You need a bath."

As soon as I turn the water on, she's naked and stepping into the tub. "It's cold," she says, cupping her vagina.

"It's going to take a minute to fill up."

She sits and stretches her legs, knees locked. "I want bubble bath," she says, but there's no more bubble bath and I'm not allowed to buy any more because it's not essential. Bubble bath is the good ole days, I tell her, and those are over, but she hasn't known any good ole days. I soap up a towel and hand it to her; the water turns gray as she slops it over her body.

"When's the last time somebody washed your hair?" I ask. She shrugs. "I know it wasn't last night, or the night before, because I bathed you." She shrugs again and holds her nose. My coworkers don't like me to wash her hair because all I can do is brush it back into a bushy ponytail, but they don't want to bathe her; they don't want to deal with her. I feel like I'm in a marriage and we have too many children and all we can do is catalogue our efforts and it all seems like too much, like more than anyone could ever expect, and we're being grossly taken advantage of.

She swishes her head from side to side. Her hair doesn't want to absorb water, not like mine. I squeeze some shampoo on top and soap it up and she wants me to play with her but I just want to get her out and dressed so I can do meds and clean the kitchen, so I can relax for an hour before the next shift comes on.

She stands and bends over, makes her anus pulse.

"Very nice," I say, "lovely. Now get out."

I bundle her in a towel and hold her like my mother used to hold me, when she called me her little papoose and rocked me before bed. I sigh and she sighs in response and I'm reminded how smart she is, too smart for a seven-year-old.

I unlock the pantry and open the medicine cabinet, shake Diamond's bottle of Adderall to see how many are left. I started taking them occasionally—though the occasions are becoming more and more frequent—because it makes the time go faster and nobody counts; we just refill the prescriptions when they run out. Along with the Adderall, Diamond takes half a yellow pill that melts on her tongue, a tiny white one she swallows with water, and a spoonful of a pink refrigerated liquid. I'm pretty sure the pink one is for her cough, though I haven't noticed her coughing. The kids always seem to be taking medicine for problems they don't have.

Diamond sits in my lap while I pass out small cups of water and pills. We were given a book that describes the

medications—side effects and proper dosage—and the director said we'd be tested but I knew we wouldn't so I didn't
bother to learn them. Had there been even the vaguest possibility of a test, I'd have studied.

There's a knock at the door and we look at each other. A
few minutes later, I'm buckling her into the backseat of a blue
sedan.

I sit next to her while my boss talks to the woman. "You'll
be back," I say, though maybe she won't this time. Maybe
she'll flourish under this specially trained foster mother.
Maybe this woman will adopt her and she'll go to college and
make good grades and have a lot of friends.

I hold her hand and we sit quietly until the woman gets in
her car and looks back at us. I don't know her name, though
I've met her a dozen times. The social workers are all pleasant and cheaply dressed and we only see them when they're
shuffling the kids around. Like the girls, I ignore them unless
I need something.

"Well," I say.

"Well," the woman says.

"Well," Diamond says, so I open the door.

She's gone five days. The only difference is she has less
stuff now.

She runs and jumps into my arms and I carry her around
the cottage on my hip. She bucks up and down and I tell her
to stop and then we sit at the kids' table and color, occasionally looking up to comment on each other's pictures. I color

the sky red and the grass blue and Strawberry Shortcake gray but I stay within the lines. Diamond colors everything the right color but doesn't stay within the lines. When we finish one, we tear it out, make a neat stack on the table.

"I want that one," Diamond says, so I give her my coloring book. She looks at the picture I was working on—Strawberry Shortcake taking a bubble bath while her cat paws at a bubble—and says she doesn't want this one, she wants another one. I sort through the shelf of coloring books she can't reach and hand her *Beauty and the Beast* and *Spider-Man* and *Blue's Clues* and they all go skidding across the floor, open-faced. Then she shoves the baby, who falls, cushioned, on her ass. The baby looks at me to confirm that something terrible has happened to her before screaming.

I drag Diamond to her room and push her in, hold the door closed while she tears it apart. There's only so much damage that can be done: chairs topple, shoes hit the wall. She sticks her fingers through the vent and reaches for my legs and says she's going to tell her daddy, that her daddy is big and mean and he is going to kill me.

"You gone die," she says.

"Okay."

"My daddy gone kill you."

"That's fine," I say, each of my responses sending her further out of control. I remember the time she was admitted to Beech Grove. I went to see her and she was bloated and looked at me like she'd never seen me before, and the nurse acted as though it was normal for a thin, energetic child to turn fat and unresponsive in the span of two weeks. After that I threatened to quit and my boss agreed to bring her back because I do certain things that the others can't, or won't.

Diamond finally tires herself out and slides to the floor, and I sit against the other side for a few minutes before letting myself in. We right her chairs and put the covers back on the beds. She puts her shoes in the closet, brings me her trash can to show me the busted plastic. Then we lie in the bed by the window, facing each other. We alternate closing our eyes, looking at each other in turns. Next month, she'll go to court and testify against her father. Already, she spends so much of her time talking to therapists about the things he has done to her. I want to take her out to my car and drive until we find a nice little house in a nice little town. We'd watch movies together at night in our pajamas and I'd forget about my husband and my growing dependence on Adderall and she'd forget about all of the bad things that have happened to her.

"Come on," I say. "Let's go outside."

I push her on the swing and she tells me to push her higher, higher. I push her so high the swing set starts jumping. When I get tired, I sit next to her and she trails her foot across the oval of dirt to slow herself before jumping off. Then she climbs into my lap, facing me, and I help get her legs into position. I'm too old to swing—it makes me nauseous—and I'm certainly too old for spider, but I hold still as she places her hands on either side of my face as if she's going to kiss me, or take my temperature, and tell her to hang on.

Back inside, I put in *The Nutty Professor* and we sit on the couch. Diamond watches the movie as if she hasn't seen it thirty times, bursting into laughter at all the right places, while I look out the window, past the pile of bikes and wagons, to the street. Whenever I tell someone I work here, they say they never see kids outside, that they didn't know kids actually lived here.

The next day I'm not working but I go in anyway and pick up Diamond. My boss doesn't care and no one else knows what goes on. I've only seen the director twice. Both times he gave us a packet to study for tests that were never administered and then went around the room asking us to toot each other's horns.

Diamond has a stain on her shirt so I take her to her room and sort through her drawers. I hold up a shirt and she shakes her head. Night shift does laundry and they never see the girls so they don't know who wears what. Finally I find a shirt that's hers, that she doesn't mind wearing, and put her in it. It's yellow with flowers around the collar and a small pocket. I give her a quarter for the pocket and then we go out to my car and I buckle her into the passenger seat of my Toyota.

She leans forward and punches buttons—1, 2, 3, 4, 5, 6—before we can hear what's playing.

"Chill out," I say, grabbing her hand.

"I want ice cream," she says.

"There's ice cream at my house." I think of all the things at my house—big-screen TVs and dozens of DVDs and fresh food, three different kinds of Blue Bell—and how they don't mean anything because I've always had them.

I park in the driveway and wave to my neighbor watering his

lawn. He's an old man who still calls black people "Negroes." I once saw him methodically drown a possum in a trash can full of water. He pulled the thing out and it was still alive so he plunged it back into the can and held it there before pulling it out again. He did it over and over, so slowly it was like a horror movie.

My husband has his straw hat on, the khaki elastic-waist shorts he always mows in. He turns the mower off and says hey and I say hey and he turns it back on. Diamond and I go inside and stand in the living room.

"Where your dog?" she asks.

"In the backyard."

We walk into the dining room and look down at the dog. She has a shock collar around her neck—a recent development. She is an unpredictable animal that barks at nothing and doesn't like people but loves other dogs and even cats. As a puppy, she seemed fine, normal even, and then she turned into a creature that scratched itself bald and would eat until it threw up and then eat that.

I had wanted a dog for years and felt certain it was my fault despite what the vet said—that some dogs are born bad, like some people.

"What her name?"

"Roxie, but I call her Shiggydiggy. She only knows one word and that's *bath*. *Shiggydiggy wanna bath?* And then she goes and hides under the bed and I have to fish her out with a broom."

We watch Roxie run up and down inside the path she has

worn, full speed, no way out. My husband hates to mow back there because it's full of shit.

I pick up the remote control and press a button, a warning sound that means if she keeps barking she's going to get shocked. The dog doesn't respond to the sound at all. She doesn't respond to the shocks, either. Despite her problems, she has a few charming qualities. Some days, before my husband gets home from work, we lie in bed and spoon. Every time I open my hard drive, she comes running to see the CD make orbs of light on the walls. When I wash dishes, she likes to watch the water ripple on the cabinets, the pots flash.

We go into the kitchen and look at the refrigerator: coloring book tear-outs with Diamond's name in jostled letters at the top, a photograph of Roxie in reindeer ears.

"It took us forever to get a couple of good ones to use as Christmas cards."

I take the rocky road from the freezer, and she eats a bowl while looking around at the cheerful wallpaper and plum-colored curtains, the clean white appliances. The woman who lived here before decorated the house and my husband moved in and then I moved in.

We listen as he comes clomping up the basement stairs and then he's standing with us in the kitchen, filling a glass with ice. His shirt is soaked through and there are flecks of grass and dirt all over him.

"What do you want to do?" I ask Diamond, who is gazing up at my husband. My husband is tall and good-looking but insecure about his looks because of his high forehead and too-thin chest. He lifts weights in the basement four times a week. He likes beer and football and reads motorcycle magazines with bikinied women on the covers, though, to my knowledge, he's never been on a motorcycle. But this makes him sound like a dick and he's not a dick, not at all. He spent weeks combing the nits out of my hair when I caught lice from one of the white girls—a tedious and time-consuming ordeal—and insisted on sleeping next to me in bed.

I drive Diamond across town to the mall; it's the kind of place I hate but drive to without thinking. There's a park next to the mall, a walking path around a lake, and sometimes I put on my tennis shoes and go there. Sit on a swing and look at the ducks. If I take the dog with me, I have to keep her on a short leash so she doesn't try to bite anyone.

At the food court, I order a box of chicken nuggets and a small Coke and we sit at a table and eat while the other children play on the plastic tree, a replica of the one at Disney World. I look around—sometimes we run into girls who are back home with their families. We talk to them with our eyes and hands when their people's backs are turned.

"I've seen the real tree," I say. "It was fake, too. I ate Moroccan food and went on a safari and there were lions and tigers and bears, oh my."

She stops chewing and cocks her head at me.

"I wish you'd been there," I say, as I help her take off her shoes.

She walks over to the tree and climbs the trunk, sticks her head out and waves before sliding down. She befriends a Mexican boy and slaps him on the ass once, good and hard, but nobody seems to mind. I move to the bench with the other parents and watch them ride a squirrel together, Diamond in front like the man. After a while, she gets bored and pushes him off and then stands and waves at me with her whole arm.

The woman next to me, a blonde in spandex, asks if she's mine and I tell her no. She's the kind of woman who comes on Wednesday nights to bring movies and popcorn. These women smile too much and won't use the bathroom, and it makes me want to steal their husbands so they can see how quickly life can rearrange itself into unfamiliar and unpleasant patterns.

"I work at a temporary shelter for abused and neglected children," I say, hating myself for wanting this woman to say I'm good, that what I am doing is a good thing.

"I bet that's very rewarding," she says.

"Not really."

I close my eyes long enough to imagine the world dark and full of noise, and then open them and find Diamond. I stare at an old man eating an ice cream cone, spinning the swirl of vanilla over his tongue. I watch him the same way he watches me—blankly, without interest—and wonder if Diamond will remember that someone loved her once, if she'll have any memory of me at all.

UPHILL

The RV park is nice and shady. The residents are mostly older and quiet, but the bugs are loud. There are all sorts of bugs and they are all so loud.

I'm sitting at the picnic table next to the trailer he has just bought, carefully avoiding the piles of bird crap while watching him fashion a wooden chute for the sewer hookup. He's impressed with himself, using nails he's found on the ground and wood from a scrap pile. Every few minutes he stops to admire his work.

"Our shit travels uphill," he says.

"That's amazing."

He sits across from me and I watch him dig around in his box full of small tools.

Before the trailer he lived on his uncle's boat, but he sank it, and before that he lived in a van in his boss's garage. When I get drunk, I yell at him and call him homeless and we don't talk for weeks but then I find myself with him again—just

a cup of coffee, just as friends—and the cycle repeats itself.
We're at the beginning of the cycle now.

"So I got this call earlier," he says. His voice has the high,
strained quality it takes on when he's lying or asking to bor-
row money. "This friend who lives in Hawaii wants me to
drive to Biloxi to take a picture of a lady."

"A picture of a lady?"

"I haven't talked to this guy in a long time."

"Who is he?"

"He sells dope," he says. "He's a bad guy."

A lot of his friends sell dope, but I've never heard him call
any of them bad guys before. "He sells weed?" I ask.

"Huge quantities of high-grade stuff. Mostly legal."

"That sounds like a bad idea."

"Yeah, it's probably a bad idea," he says.

I'm surprised to hear him agree with me. He stops digging
around in his box. I turn a page in my magazine. "How much
did he offer to pay you?"

"He said to name my price. I was thinking a thousand."

"A thousand? If someone tells you to name your price you
don't say a thousand. Did you tell him you couldn't do it?"

"I said I'd call him back."

"Why didn't you tell him you couldn't do it?" If I wasn't
here, or we were in a fight, he would already be on his way
down there.

"I'm not gonna do it."

"They're going to kill that woman," I say, because I want
to hear what it sounds like. I want him to say no, they're not,

but he doesn't. There she is—eating a tunafish sandwich or watching a game show on TV, not knowing she will soon be dead. It's kind of thrilling. I wonder what she looks like, if she's pretty.

"I'll call him right now with you sitting there and tell him I can't do it. I'm going to have to make some stuff up."

"Of course, make some stuff up. I don't care." I flip another page in my magazine, a *Cosmopolitan* from November 2002. I found a whole stack of them in his Laundromat. "Wait," I say. "Hold on a second."

"What?"

"Let's think about this for another minute." This is not my life, or it is not the life I'm supposed to be living, and so I can pretend that it is. I don't consider the actuality of my situation, which is that every day I live this life it becomes more and more mine, the real one, and the one I'm supposed to be living falls further away; eventually it will be gone forever. "Whether or not you take the picture, somebody's going to do it and the woman'll be dead, right?"

"That's right," he says.

"So either way she's dead and all he wants you to do is take a picture. And you're broke."

"I'm not broke."

He takes a sip of his beer, the beer I bought. I know exactly how much money he has because he empties his pockets out on the counter as soon as he gets home, balled-up ones and fives, sometimes a couple of twenties. He never has more than fifty dollars on him.

"People take my picture all the time," I say. "Every time I go through a toll road my picture gets taken."

"Not really the same thing. And when are you going through toll roads?"

"Are you sure he doesn't want you to do anything else?"

"No, just the picture."

"Your child support's late," I say, though we don't talk about his children, who live in Virginia (a state he is not allowed to enter for reasons that remain unclear). I can just assume he hasn't paid it. He has no bank account. When someone writes him a check, I have to cash it for him because he lost his ID, sunk to the bottom of the lake along with the boat.

"You think I should do it?" he says. "I can't believe you think I should do it."

"For two thousand."

"Are you serious?"

"You'd do it if I wasn't here."

"No I wouldn't."

"Then why didn't you tell him no right off?"

"Because he's my friend—I was going to think about it first. I owe him that much."

"Well call him back and tell him you'll do it. And I get to come."

"No, babe. I'm not involving you in that kind of stuff."

"I'm coming," I say, "and that's final." He seems pleased and I wonder if this is what he wanted all along, if I'm stupid. We stay together, I tell myself, because the sex is so good; if the sex weren't so good, I would have broken this cycle a long time ago.

He calls the guy back and makes affirmative-sounding noises while I watch him pace. So many of my boyfriends have been pacers—it must make them feel important. He says fifteen and gestures for a pen. I hand him one and he scrawls an upside-down address on my magazine, a phone number and the name Susan Lacey. I went to school with some identical twins named Lacey. They were of average intelligence and attractiveness so no one seemed to know what to do with them.

I gather my stuff and climb the two steps into the trailer. I'm still not used to the dimensions—the narrowness of the doors, how small everything is. There are booby traps everywhere, sharp edges that need to be filed down, cabinets that fall open when you walk by. Only in the bed do I feel my normal size.

I open the closet and a light comes on; it is his favorite feature. I shove my clothes back into my overnight bag, my toothbrush and toothpaste and foaming facial cleanser. We'll have to go by my apartment to get my camera because he doesn't have one. I wish he had his own damn camera and find myself getting angry about all of the things he doesn't have and how he assumes I will provide them. I sit on the bed with its ugly pilled comforter that probably came with the trailer and look at my arms, the finger-shaped bruises. *I'm going to be involved in a murder,* I think. There is no voice that tells me to stop, that says what I am doing is wrong. I can't remember if there ever was a voice. I don't remember a voice.

. . .

I refuse to let him take my car so we clean out the truck he uses for work, which belongs to his boss. There's a situation with a headlight that is an illegal blue color; the cops have already pulled him over twice and told him to get it fixed. We pour two beers into giant McDonald's cups and he rolls a joint for the road, all of which is worrisome but I tell myself we're embarking upon a great adventure.

I settle myself into the passenger seat, kick trash around the floorboard.

We pass a group of men near the entrance and he rolls down his window. They are born-again bikers, men with lots of tattoos and angry faces, but they don't drink or do drugs or get into fights; they show up at trials to support children who have been abused, stand in the back of the courtroom with their arms crossed. They're biker angels, he tells me, making fun of them, but I think it's what they call themselves.

At my apartment, he waits in the truck while I walk the three flights upstairs. I get my camera and a pair of shorts and a bikini; the bottoms can double as panties. I wander the rooms wondering what else I might need, if I should just lock the door, put on my pajamas and get in bed. It looks so comfortable, the sheets newly changed, sage green—such a pleasant color. I grab a bottle of water and a couple of Luna bars and then we're on the highway, headed south. I haven't been to Biloxi since I broke up with Richard. I have so many old boyfriends now, spread out all over, and so many things remind me of them. I'll pass a Wendy's and remember the one who would only eat plain hamburgers. There we are, sitting under the yellow lights with our trays in front of us as I eat one french fry at a time. Nearly every movie, every song and TV show and item of food reminds me of someone and it is a horrible way to live.

I flip down the visor to look at myself. My hair's in a ratty ponytail and I don't have any makeup on and I'm too old to be going around barefaced, my mother says. I wish I'd showered before we left his trailer but it's so small the water runs everywhere and I can't turn around without the curtain touching my arms or legs, the same curtain that touched the arms and legs of a stranger.

"I brought my swimsuit in case there's a pool at our hotel." He puts a hand on my knee. "I need a new one—this one's from three summers ago and it's all worn on the butt."

"I'll get you a new one," he says. "I'll get you a white bikini so I can see your nipples." The word *bikini* doesn't sound right in his mouth. And he hardly ever buys me anything, though it's always his pot we smoke and I've never once bought condoms. Condoms are expensive, he tells me, especially the way we go through them. He has never suggested we don't use them, though, which is nice of him.

"Do you want me to drive?" I ask.

"I'm fine."

"I haven't had as much to drink."

"I'm fine," he says again.

"Did the guy say what he wanted the pictures for?"

"We know why he wants them."

"I know but did he say it?"

"No."

"'Cause that's not how it works."

"Right," he says. He turns the radio up. We both like country music. We also like rap. No one knows where I am. When I'm with him, I don't return my friends' text messages or answer my mother's phone calls. I fall down a rabbit hole.

It's not a bad drive down 49. There are plenty of places to stop, which I appreciate, and lots of antique malls made out of connecting storage units. My mother used to make me go to them with her back when I was too young to refuse, but I don't remember her ever buying anything. I wonder what she was looking for. There's a catfish house shaped like an igloo and another one in a massive barn, only about five miles apart. I like the men on the side of the highway selling fruits and vegetables, nice-looking men in overalls, real country people. We live in Mississippi and almost everyone we know is from Mississippi but we don't know any real country people.

"I have to pee," I say, "just stop wherever, whenever it's convenient." He tells me I pee too much, and it's true, I do pee a lot. I close my eyes and think about the woman, Susan Lacey. I imagine her in a shapeless housedress and heavy shoes with rubber soles like a nurse, spooning fro-yo from a gallon container. And then I imagine a younger Susan Lacey, her hair long and dark, eyes full of life. She's on the street, carrying a recyclable bag full of organic fruits and vegetables, flowers sticking out of the top of it. The picture will capture her mid-stride, head turning to look for cars as she crosses the street. It's a picture I've seen so many times on the crime shows I watch, the photograph snapping the color out of everything.

"Can I smoke?" I ask.

"I don't care."

"No, the joint."

"Let's wait till after," he says.

I say okay but after feels like forever. I wish I'd grabbed a book from my apartment—all I have is the *Cosmo* with the address and number on it and I've already read it from cover to cover. I reread an interview with Cameron Diaz. *Cosmo* asks her what the secret is to being an effective flirt—"Is it 'flipping your goddamn hair,' like Lucy Liu advised you to do in *Angels*?" And Cameron Diaz says, "Yes, flip the goddamn hair [laughs]. I think the secret is trying to be charming. I always try to make a man laugh, and usually, it's by making fun of myself." I wonder if her answer would be different in 2013, if she would say something so embarrassing and unfeminist-like. I try to focus on the trees, the way the light filters through them, but there's Susan Lacey again—she is definitely the younger, dark-haired one. Perhaps she's even beautiful, but it isn't going to save her.

Less than three hours later, we're here. He pulls into a gas station and I slip my card into the slot before he can ask and go inside, buy a 16-ounce beer and a king-size Twix.

He's still pumping when I come back out, talking on his burner. I get in the truck and take off my flip-flops—my toenails bright red, so pretty.

He hands me a receipt, which I let fall to the floor without looking at it. I type the address into my phone, direct him through the city. For some reason the sound isn't working and I can't get it to work even though the media volume is turned all the way up.

"Don't you have a boyfriend that lives here?" he asks. He knows I have an ex-boyfriend who lives here. He lives in a high-rise apartment and drives a black Mercedes with a personalized license plate that means supreme ruler in some Asian language. He is a horrible person who made me go to church with him on Sundays, a Californian, a former marine, a drunk. I have no idea where I find these people.

"No," I say.

He looks at me.

"That was like three years ago."

"When's the last time you talked to him?"

"Not since we broke up," I say. "Richard."

"Dick," he says, "that's right, good old *Dick*."

"Let's talk about your ex-girlfriends. Were they all ugly? Make a left at the next light."

"I don't date ugly chicks."

"You know I've met a lot of the girls you dated?"

He sighs because I'm right—they were all weirdly tall or hook-nosed; one of them had so many tattoos she looked deranged. "How much further?" he asks.

"Farther."

"Okay," he says, "Jesus Christ. How much farther?"

"Three miles. If he has her address, why's he need a picture? Why doesn't he just send somebody there to kill her?"

"We're going to her job," he says, and then, "Hey, babe? Could you just stop talking for just a minute?"

We pull into the parking lot of an Office Depot. "Is this it?" he asks.

"This is the address you wrote down."

Office Depots depress me and I refuse to get out. I open my bag and hand him the camera, turn it on and off. "This button here," I say. "I hope she's in there and we can get this over with. I want to go swimming, and maybe gamble. I love to gamble." I've decided I'll definitely rent a room at a casino, a nice one, and order room service and drink overpriced drinks at the hotel bar and fuck him in a huge bed with too many pillows.

I watch his back as he walks into the store: stocky and bald-headed, tattoos covering his thick arms. He's not attractive in the conventional way but he makes beautiful babies. I'll never have a baby with him but I like the idea of it, having a small version of him that I could control, who would listen to me and obey me and tell me every thought that popped into his head. The doors slide open and he's gone, disappeared into the sadness of Office Depot forever. The turn of events deflates me.

Ten minutes later, he gets back in the truck.

"So?"

"No Suzie."

"What took you so long?"

"I bought some envelopes," he says, and tosses the bag to the floor. He hands me the camera and I immediately check to see if he took any pictures; he didn't. I turn it off. "What now?"

"I don't know. Let me think for a minute."

"Drive us to a nice hotel and I'll rent a room and we can pretend we're on a stakeout. Set up a command center."

"This isn't a game," he says, pulling out of the lot. "It's not a fucking game."

He drives in an angry silence. When someone is mad at me, I don't know what to do except be mad back. He drives fast, like he knows where he's going, and I don't ask. When he decides to talk to me, I won't be ready to talk to him, I tell myself, and it makes me feel better but then I start thinking about all the things I want to say. Every one of them is a question. I look out the window as he drives and I have no idea where he's going or what we're doing. I want to be inside his head for one minute, just one minute so I can get ahead of him, or at least not feel so behind. We could be here to kill Susan Lacey, for all I know, though I don't think he would do that for fifteen hundred dollars but maybe it's fifteen thousand and then I'd go to prison as an accessory because they wouldn't believe me, they never do. I'd get five years, at least, even if all my people pooled their money to get me the best lawyer.

I tell him I have to pee again and he pulls into a gas station, throws the truck into park so fast it lurches. In the bathroom, I wash my hands, splash water on my face. I look at myself in the mirror and think, *Fuck you. Fuck you, you fuckup.* I think all my problems might be solved if I could look in the mirror and see my ugliness reflected back at me.

As I'm purchasing a six-pack, my phone rings and I know it's my mother so I don't answer. I don't even look. She'll call again in twenty minutes or half an hour and ask what I am doing, if I'm okay. She always wants to know if I'm okay, if I'm happy, which makes it impossible to talk to her.

"Where are we going?" I ask as coldly as possible.

"I'm dropping you off at my father's house," he says. "You can spend the night there."

"Oh no, I'm not going there. I don't know your father."

"You'll be fine," he says. "It's safe there."

"Why? What's going on?"

"I have to find this woman."

"I know, that's why we're here. We have to find her so let's find her."

"You don't understand," he says.

"You're right, I don't. Explain it to me."

I open a beer and he takes it out of my hand. I open another. I tell him I am not, under any circumstances, going to sit and watch TV with some old man I don't know. An old man he hates and doesn't talk to. I had forgotten that his father even lived here. I tell him to take me to a hotel but he doesn't take me to his father's house or to a hotel. He takes me to a bar. We get out and I follow him inside. It's not the kind of place we frequent—a fancy wine bar with too many mirrors, where I feel underdressed and greasy. The Office Depot girl wouldn't be here.

I sit next to him on a barstool and he orders his usual: a Budweiser and a shot of Jameson. I order a gin martini, dirty. The olives are pierced through a long wooden stick, danger-ous, and I eat them carefully, one at a time, and remember that there are pleasures in life; sometimes they're so small they shouldn't compensate for all of the shit, but they do.

They really do. Once the olives are gone, I look up hotel reviews on my phone even though I know where I want to stay: The Hard Rock. There are young, good-looking people there and they let you bring your dog.

"Hey, babe," he says. "Hey, love." I don't look at him. Other women may do their best to be nice and accommodating but I try to be as unlikeable as possible, test men too soon. The right one will love me for it, I imagine, though I've been through enough to know that the right one doesn't exist, this perfect man who will be whole yet malleable, who will allow me to be as ugly as I want.

Twenty minutes later, I'm in a hotel room by myself: two beds, a large bathroom with an array of soaps and lotions, everything perfectly beige. It's on the fourteenth floor over-looking the Gulf and I stand in the window and try to make out the barrier islands: Cat Island, Ship, Horn, some other one I forget. In '69, Camille split Ship Island in two.

It's not the first time I've waited for him in a hotel room. I've given up so much to be with him and some of these things are for the best. He has taught me sex without love, a Buddhist's degree of unattachment. He's taught me that I can only rely on myself and it's a good lesson, one I needed to learn. He also taught me to drive a stick shift and put cream cheese on sandwiches, an appreciation of westerns. Everyone leaves something behind; there are so many things I wouldn't have if I hadn't had all of them.

I know he'll show up in the morning when it's time to check out and it'll be done: the picture taken, cash in hand, an inexplicably large amount unaccounted for. I call room service and order a bacon cheeseburger with fries and a strawberry milkshake and eat everything including most of the condiments in their fat little jars. Then I lie in bed and watch the most boring thing I can find on TV—old women selling garish jewelry and elastic waist pantsuits—and the longer I watch, the more I begin to imagine a world in which these things might appeal to me.

I call my mother; I can't help it. She always answers, even if she's with her priest or in the movie theater.

"Hello?" she says. "Who's this?"

"Mom? Are you there?"

"I was asleep," she says. "I fell asleep. What time is it?"

"Eight o'clock." I don't know why I called her but I do it constantly, against my will. More often even than she calls me. I call her because she is there, because she loves me, and because one day she'll die and I won't know how to live in a world without her in it. I don't know how to live in this one.

When we hang up, I look at my phone: three minutes and twenty-seven seconds. It seemed like so much longer.

Sometime during the night, he comes in. I pretend to sleep as he takes off his clothes and gets into bed, reaches a cold hand beneath my shirt.

"Tell me," I say, swatting his hand away. "What happened?"

"I got it."

"Where's my camera?"

"On the dresser."

"What'd you do?"

"It was nothing," he says. "It was easy."

"But what'd you do? What happened?" I ask, knowing I'll never know what happened. I'll never know what he does when I'm not with him. When I'm alone I don't do anything the least bit interesting. He tugs at my panties and I help him, kick them to the end of the bed. I run my hand over his prickly head because it's what I like best about him. But once I'm safe inside my apartment, I won't answer his calls or listen to his voice mails. I'll watch him through the peephole until he goes away and if he acts crazy I'll document his behavior and get a restraining order. I'll tell Farrell, the apartment manager, to keep a lookout and she'll be happy to be given this assignment—she loves a purpose, someone she might yell at as she hobbles around the parking lot on her crutches. I'll even move if I have to, to Texas or North Carolina, somewhere far enough away that he won't bother to find me unless a bad man calls and offers him money and he's the only bad man I can say for sure I know. This is not my life. It isn't the one, I tell myself, as I wrap my legs around him as tightly as possible.

DIRTY

They all want videos. This one bought a digital camera with his tax refund and films me in bed, doing things to him, while he watches the screen. He asks me questions—do you like this? do you like this?—answering for me when I grow unresponsive. I notice the soles of my feet are dirty. I don't know how they got so dirty, I've been inside all day: padding around on his carpet, heating up soup and watching television.

"Do you like choking on my cock?" he asks.

I look into the camera and say no and after that he's irritated because I've messed up his video and this one was on target to be a good one. I'd done everything right, acted just like a whore. It's taking forever so I get on top and ride him until he's about to come, then hop off and watch him make a mess on his belly.

"That's a ton," I say. Boys like to hear things like this. I hand him a wad of Kleenex and he wipes his stomach, the hairs sticking together to form a little peak.

We get dressed and go to China Buffet 2.

I fill a plate and set it at the table, my Sprite already there. I go back for an egg roll, cream cheese fried wontons, slices of cantaloupe, a bowl of ice cream. I nod at the Chinese girls as I pass. There are real Chinese people here, not like at the other place in the old Shoney's.

He tucks his napkin into his shirt like his fat father and eyeballs me. He knows I won't eat half of it. He knows I won't eat much of anything even though I carry chocolate bars in my purse, packages of cookies and honey roasted peanuts.

"What are you looking at?" I ask, as I pick the egg and bits of carrot out of my fried rice, sip my Sprite. The Chinese girl comes over and tops it off. "Take your plate away?" she asks him. He tells her he's still working on it. There's a half a chicken stick and some shreds of cabbage.

When we get back to his house, he goes into the other bedroom to play guitar and smoke a joint. My sister smoked a bunch of his pot once and said it was Mexican dirt weed. She says I'm not allowed to smoke his dirt weed or ride on the back of his motorcycle because I'll fall off and hit my head and my brains will spill all over the pavement. She acts like my mother even though I already have a mother. She knows I'll listen to her because I know she knows how things are in a way my mother will never know. I want to talk to her but she's still in the hospital so I call my friend Iris.

I tell her I'm not sucking dick on camera anymore, her baby crying in the background.

"It can't be good," she says. "What good can come of it?"

"I don't know—sometimes we watch it together and it turns us on."

"It doesn't turn you on," she says, and I tell her she's right, it doesn't, but the idea of it does. "Ideas are useless," she says, "as soon as you have one you forget it. I read self-help books and I'm fixed for like a day—for a day I'm not putting my shit on anybody and I'm only thinking good thoughts and the next day everything's fucked again." The baby is wailing now. "I have to go," she says, "little man's hungry. You should see my tits, they're so big. You're going to end up on the internet so stop, just stop."

I go to the bathroom and brush my teeth. I need a new toothbrush. This one is shitty because it came from the dentist.

My boyfriend starts a new song and I pause to hear what it is—"Folsom Prison." He tries to sound exactly like Johnny Cash, which bothers me because he has no imagination but he thinks he's a fucking genius because he's registered with BMI. Ryan Ellington's BMI card is stuck to the bottom right-hand corner of the bathroom mirror. I bet Ryan Ellington is hot. I wipe a little foamy spit on it and then get in his bed, on the side that's mine, the side that doesn't have a table to set things on, and pull the spread up to my chin. It's black and gray with a stripy animal print circa 1989. It has linty balls all over it, which I pick off and release between the bed and wall.

"I'm about to feed the fish," he says, from the doorway.

"I'm sleeping."

"Come watch."

"I don't want to," I say, but then he's mad, so I get up and go in there and sit on a foldout chair next to the table with all his drug stuff on it: a wooden box with spiky metal teeth, rolling papers, a yellow plastic lighter and a Zippo, an ashtray littered with roaches. I want a cigarette but I'd have to go outside to smoke it.

He has live crickets in a mesh bucket, which he drops into the tank two at a time. The fish open their mouths and eat them off the top of the water: *bloop!* The fish are too small for eating but too big to be in a tank. He got them out of the river. I don't like the river because there are gars and snakes and the water makes you feel all crackly and tight when it dries on your skin but I go with him because his ex-girlfriend never went with him once in four years and I don't want to be like her. She once prostituted herself behind a Blockbuster Video. There are also some snails and a crawfish. The crawfish is a monster. I like to watch him eat the fish when they die because it goes on forever unless you fall asleep.

"Do you want to feed them?" he asks.

"They smell awful."

"Come on, just one."

I reach my hand in and they jump all over it.

"You complain a lot."

"I'm difficult," I say, though I don't know if I'm difficult because I don't know how difficult other girls are. He says I'm more difficult than most, though not as difficult as the Blockbuster girl, but he also says it's okay because I'm pretty and pretty girls have room, unlike fat girls, like my sister, who have no room, who should learn to keep their mouths shut.

I grab one and throw it in, right above a fish's mouth: *bloop!* Then I turn around and walk out, wash my hands and get back in bed. Adult Swim is on. They aren't shows I'd have ever watched on my own but I like them now, especially the one with the mean baby and talking dog. I feel like I'm figuring something out about boys when I watch them—something like how much they can appreciate smart when it's presented to them as stupid.

He takes off all his clothes and gets into bed with me. I put my head on his shoulder and stick my face in his armpit; even when he stinks I like it, especially when he stinks. I'm allergic to his semen, though. It burns and gives me infections, but he always wants to put it in me because he has this notion about "spilled seed." Anything outside the vagina constitutes spilled. I tell him I'm going to get pregnant but he knows this isn't true because I'm on the pill and the pill is 99.9 percent effective if you take it every day, which I do. I also have a tilted uterus.

In the morning, he wakes me at six-thirty and then gets in the shower. I stand in front of the refrigerator listening to him sing "Ramblin' Man." He likes to picture himself on the open road with his guitar strapped to his back but he never goes anywhere. To guarantee he stays put, he buys property that poor people live in. He owns a whole little neighborhood of nine houses that should be condemned. I help him clean them out when the poor people pick up and move in the middle of the night and he pays me in buffets, hot showers, and a warm place to sleep because I don't work, which is temporary, my not working, but the longer I don't work the less I can imagine going back to my cubicle at the government office where I used to take disability claims, reinstating prisoners' benefits while they gawked.

I'm careful not to burn the toast because he won't eat it if there's any black on it. Then I slab on butter and jelly while a couple of eggs fry. When the eggs look about done, I top them with pepperjack and cheddar and he makes a sandwich out of the whole thing and eats it while standing over the sink. I sit on the counter and watch, kick my legs—the yolks squirt and dribble because I didn't cook them long enough, he could get salmonella—and think about my day, all the empty hours and how I don't even have enough money to go to lunch, how he didn't leave me any money on the piano bench yesterday like he sometimes does. I wipe a glob of yellow off his beard and he picks up his briefcase and kisses me goodbye. After I lock the door behind him, I think how much I love him, how he is like a husband and I am like a wife.

I spend the day waiting for him, but I force myself to do a few things so I'll have something to tell him when he asks what I did. I jumped rope five hundred times. I read to page 38 in my library book. I cleaned the bathtub and took a bath.

When he gets home, I want to go somewhere, the drive-in maybe, but he wants me to handcuff him to the bed. All day long he's been in charge and now he wants somebody else to be in charge. I like handcuffing him to the bed for a few minutes, while I sit on his face, but then I want to leave him there and go cut my toenails or watch television. I don't want to do the things he wants me to do to him.

I slap him hard and call him the names he likes—bitch, whore, cunt. He tosses his head from side to side like you never see anyone do in real life. It reminds me of a princess trapped in a tower. I slap him again and work my finger into his asshole and think about what I'm going to eat for supper because there's nothing to eat here that I like. He doesn't even have any milk. If he'd give me some money, I'd go buy milk. Then I could eat cereal.

"Please," he says, "please." More head tossing.

"Don't beg," I say, "I hate for a man to beg," but he thinks this is part of the program so he bites his lip. I slap him hard and scoot to the edge of the bed and look at him out of the corner of my eye, which I imagine is pretty creepy. If I were him and he were me, I'd be creeped out.

"I'm going to leave you here," I say.

He looks at me like a dog, uncomprehending, whatever I say goes. I put my panties on and close the door. In the kitchen, I wash my hands and listen to the wheelchair man roll around, the laugh track on his television erupt. The house is split into three pieces: my boyfriend (slumlord) on one end, the wheelchair man in the middle, and a pretty white girl who talks black on the other end. Sometimes she comes over and wants to wash her clothes and I tell her I'm sorry, I was on my way out, but then I have to leave, which really pisses me off.

I turn on the big-screen in the den. Like everything else, he got it for free or cheap and there's something wrong with it. In this case, the picture is usually shaped like a bow tie. Right now it's not but it could go into bow tie mode at any minute. I lie on the fake leather couch and watch *Man vs. Wild*, nestle my feet into a pile of blankets. So far nothing has proven useful—it's doubtful I'll ever have a reason to make my pants into a flotation device. On day five in the middle of nowhere, Bear is lying on the ground in the pitch dark talking about how hungry he is, and then he's talking about how lonely he is. Just about everyone seems to need my love and it makes me sad because already my love has been spread around too much and there are still so many people I might have saved who will now be lost forever.

My boyfriend is hollering from the bedroom—he has to take a piss. I go into the kitchen and look through the cabinets and there's still nothing, and then I remember the pint of ice cream in the freezer. There's a lot left but I already picked out all the heath bar chunks so it's barely worth eating. I take the top off and put the carton in the microwave, slurp it from a big spoon while Bear finds his way back to civilization.

I fall asleep. When I wake up, it's dark. I like it when this happens. I twist my hair into a bun on top of my head and walk quietly back to the bedroom and open the door.

"You fucking bitch," he says, without looking at me.

I make like I'm going to walk out and he turns and says, "No—you're not a bitch, you're a smart, beautiful woman." I can't stand to be called a woman. I'm a girl. I'll always be a girl. I take the little key and unlock him and he runs to the bathroom and pees for a long time, a heavy stream. Tomorrow is Saturday and we'll go to the river and drink beer and maybe catch more fish to put in the tank. Some of them will die from shock and then the monster will have a heyday. I think about this and try to get excited. He goes into the kitchen so I follow him in there and kneel on the linoleum. He gags me again and again until I throw up a small pool of sour vanilla. Now he's happy. Now he will do whatever I want, he says. I want to see my sister. I want to eat Thai food with her at our favorite place where we used to live but I can't because she's in the hospital and we don't live there anymore.

I scoop up the mess with a paper towel and stay on the floor.

"So?" he says, opening a can of Diet Rite. With his other hand, he pets the top of my head.

Second choice would be the drive-in, where I'd fall asleep in his arms before the double feature begins, but then I think about the last time we went to the drive-in, how he had a taillight out and we got pulled over and he wasn't wearing any underwear so he couldn't tuck his one-hitter into his crotch like he usually does so he told me to put it in my panties but I refused and we were pushing it back and forth while the policeman was walking toward us and then he shoved it between his ass cheeks at the last second. The cop asked him to get out and the two of them walked around the car to look at the taillight and when he finally got back in, he said, I know not to ever consider your panties again and I said, No, please don't consider them, and then I had to drink myself out of a panic attack while he laughed and took a single shot of whiskey, like every time he comes back from Murfreesboro with a slab of marijuana in his motorcycle jacket.

"I wonder what Coach is doing," I say, though I know what Coach is doing—getting drunk on his couch. When he gets really drunk, he'll spy on his neighbors or hide things from himself around the house. Coach is the only person we hang out with, a bad alcoholic with a cough like he's dying.

We drive over there with half a bottle of whiskey and a six-pack and he answers the door in his sunglasses.

"Miss Amy," he says.

"Nice hat," I say. He's wearing a cap with a pile of fake shit on the brim. Shithead, it says. I know a girl gave it to him, the fat one he's having sex with but won't take out of the house. He makes her park in back so nobody can see her car.

I put my beer in the refrigerator and sit on one of two couches. There are also two televisions. Right now there's baseball on one and *Seinfeld* on the other. Coach rolls a joint and they smoke it. This is called a "safety meeting." They text each other back and forth: safety meeting? safety meeting? because you can't text things like *let's get together and smoke some dope*.

Coach deals three stacks of cards and we take turns tossing them into an upturned cowboy hat under the baseball TV. Whoever lands the most is due a quarter from everybody playing. Except me, I don't pay. My cards fly everywhere.

"Will you fix me a drink?" Coach asks. This is new. We wait to see what I'll say. I don't say anything but I walk over to him and take his empty glass.

"Not too much water," he says.

I go into the kitchen, which is full of to-go boxes and plastic forks and other things boys have trouble throwing out, and fill his glass almost all the way with whiskey and add a splash of water. He used to drink it with Coke but it exacerbated his psoriasis. His legs are red and scaly and he always wears shorts. It's an admirable quality, I think, showcasing one's most glaring defect.

He compliments me on my drink-making skills and we watch *Seinfeld* without the sound. George, Jerry, Elaine, and

Kramer are sitting around a booth at the diner, drinking coffee and not eating. Then Kramer throws up his hands and
walks out. Then it's back to Jerry's apartment where Jerry
is talking on the enormous landline. I think about pizza—I
could suggest we order pizza and they'd say okay and it would
come and I wouldn't touch it, or I'd eat five slices and it still
wouldn't be enough.

I smoke because I can and think about what Coach will do
when we leave, if the fat girl'll come over and make him late-
night snacks or try to get him off.

There's a knock at the door. We look at each other and
don't move. Finally, I stand but Coach gets up and puts his
arm out like he's going to take care of it so I sit back down.
Of course it's the fat girl, who I've never met, never even seen.
All I know is that she does all of the work of a girlfriend but
gets none of the reward. He tells her he has company and she
asks if she can join us and he says no because he's busy and
she starts crying and then the door closes so we can't hear
what they're saying.

"Why won't he just let her come in?"

My boyfriend says it's not our business, so I tell him I want
pizza and he gets out his cell phone and orders what I like
and I don't think he'd ever put me on the internet so I should
just stop worrying about it. I should let him keep his videos.
I like how skinny my face looks when sucking dick, from that
angle. I look strung-out, crack whore. My boyfriend is sweet,
though. He orders me pizza and takes me out in public and
when I say I want to go home, he takes me home. I could rest

my head on his shoulder and he'd kiss it, no matter who was around. I'm so lucky.

The fat girl drives off, taking out a garbage can, maybe, and Coach comes back in and sits down.

"We don't care if you're fucking a fat girl," I say.

"I'm not fucking her," he says.

"Of course you are."

We throw another round of cards and then the pizza comes and I take a pill that Coach gives me even though my boyfriend doesn't like for me to take pills because the Blockbuster girl took a lot of pills. She was a pillhead and he has no respect for pillheads. She spent all her money on pills and didn't respect her body. I don't respect my body, either, but I tell him I do. I tell him I wish I'd been a virgin when we'd met and he was the only person I'd ever been with, stuff like that.

We hear a car followed by a loud series of knocks, and the fat girl comes barging in wearing sweatpants with elastic around the ankles, her hair in a banana clip. I haven't seen a banana clip in a long time, but it's a nice look. Maybe if I could get a bunch of people to start wearing banana clips we could bring them back.

"I'm Amy," I say, and hold my hand up, though she's just a few feet away.

"Ginger," she says.

Coach laughs his hoarse crazy laugh and deals four stacks and she sits next to him and calls him a shithead. She taps the bill over his eyes and he takes the cap off and throws it across the room. Help yourself to some pizza, he says to her, and my boyfriend and I look at each other. He puts an arm around me and I feel solid, like we are the model for a good life and happiness by comparison, which is how everything is measured.

We take turns tossing cards into the hat and the fat girl wins and it's decided that I have to pay because she doesn't want to sleep with me and therefore I can't stiff her. I take a quarter from my purse and hand it over and she's happy and gloating and I wonder how she can get out of bed in the morning without wanting to die she's so fat and not the kind of fat girl where people are always commenting on how pretty her face is, either. She goes into the kitchen and comes back with a plate with one slice on it, eats it daintily with a napkin on her leg. I ask my boyfriend to take me home.

When I wake up, I can tell it's sunny outside, a good day for the river, but I don't feel like going to the river. I don't feel like getting out of bed. I miss my ex-boyfriend, I think, and this feels right, but there are so many of them now and I'm not sure which one I miss. Lately I'm running one behind so I only stop missing the last one when the current becomes the ex and then I miss him so I'm never fully with the one I'm with, which is maybe why they keep leaving me.

I look at my boyfriend—eye boogers, dried spit around his mouth—and know I'll miss him, too. I'll miss the orgasms he gives me, and how he smells, and I'll be sad I didn't accidentally get pregnant while I had the chance.

I get up and go to the bathroom and wash my face. Then I

go into the kitchen and take a Diet Rite from the refrigerator, drink it while putting on my sports bra and tennis shoes.

The wheelchair man is parked in the sun. He's about my age, but seems a lot older. I know he's in a wheelchair because he was drunk driving and got into an accident and killed somebody, which is something that could have happened to me many nights but hasn't. I wonder if his dick works, if it would help if I sucked it. He nods and says hello (hello!) and I walk to the end of the driveway and then I start running. I wasn't planning on running but I know he's watching me. I run as fast as I can until I reach the main road and then turn around and run back, thinking *faster, faster.* I think: *When I get to that stump, that mailbox, that car, I can stop,* but I run past all of them.

He's still there so I stop and lean against the brick wall to catch my breath.

"I should really stop smoking," I say, but I don't like the way it sounds, like a lie, so I say, "No, I'm just out of shape."

"I see you jumping rope out here every day," he says.

"I'm a little hungover."

The wheelchair man has found God, or maybe we just assume this because the church pays three-quarters of his rent every month.

"I used to drink," he says, "you probably know that. I'd get into fights a lot."

"Did you win?"

"Nobody ever really wins."

"So you lost."

"No," he says, and he looks up into the trees like I am boring him completely so I tell him I'll see him later, and he says,
"Have a nice day," and I go inside and finish my Diet Rite
and wonder what he thinks about me, a pretty girl who jumps
rope and doesn't work even though she has two legs that can
run so fast.

In the bedroom, I lie on top of my boyfriend but he doesn't
budge so I go back to the kitchen and get out the bacon. The
bacon smell will wake him up and then we'll eat breakfast and
start drinking beer and I'll feel better.

His phone rings. Right when it's about to go to voice mail
he answers it in his radio voice with the joyless laugh that
stupid people find charming. It's one of his tenants who can't
pay his rent and my boyfriend is explaining the late procedure to him, probably for the tenth time, because it involves
advanced math and lawn mowing. There's an even more
complicated procedure for when they can't afford to pay the
deposit. He learned them from his dad, who is also a slumlord, and the procedures don't make sense but they sound so
completely rational that the person always comes to the con-
clusion that they're not only bad with money but also an idiot.
It's how he makes me feel a lot of times but so far I haven't
been able to come up with any hard evidence.

He walks into the kitchen naked. I pour him a glass of
Kool-Aid and he takes a seat and repeats what I've just overheard him say to Mr. James. He tells me he likes it when
they're a few days late but he doesn't like it when they just
don't pay, which I already know. When they're a few days late,
he gets an extra fifty dollars. It makes me kind of sad because

that extra fifty dollars only ensures they'll be late again next
month and then they're out another fifty, or a hundred. It's
how my parents handle money, always behind, paying twice
as much for everything. I put four pieces of bread in the
toaster while the bacon pops and he digs a finger in his ear
and looks at it.

After we eat he goes to the bathroom and reads *Siddhartha*, which is the only book he'll read and only on the toilet,
while I put beer in the cooler. He's too cheap to buy ice so we
have to use a ton of trays, pop the cubes out a handful at a
time and be sure to refill them for the next time.

Coach comes in without knocking and lies on the floor.
"I'm dying," he says. He goes into a coughing fit and places
his hand on his chest and I'm sure his insides are all black and
scabby even though he's only thirty-two. I don't want him to
die but if he did, then maybe something would be different.
I step over him to throw a can away and go back to my trays.
He stands and leans against the counter, pulls the flask from
his pants. I didn't know he was coming with us but I don't
care. The two of them go off to hunt turtles while I lay out, or
scoop up stuff with my net.

"Your girlfriend spend the night?" I ask.

"She's not my girlfriend."

"Okay, your *friend with benefits*."

"Why do you torture me like this, Miss Amy?"

"Why do you call me Miss Amy, Coach? A title of respect
for fucking your best friend?"

"Something like that," he says, and lets the screen door
slam shut. It makes him nervous when I say *fuck*.

. . .

We stop at the gas station for another twelve-pack and some snacks and then drop Coach's truck off at the pull-out. Then we drive back to the put-in and I stand around in my bikini while they carry the canoes down to the water where a Mexican family is fishing and remember the time my friend Travis asked me what I was still doing in this town, like I was too good for this place.

I carry my paddle and life jacket down to our canoe and he holds it steady while I step in. Once we're situated, I paddle hard so my boyfriend won't have to tell me to—I know he wants to get away from the Mexicans before we start drinking—and stop when I hit thirty strokes. I ask him to hand me a beer and rest my paddle across my legs while I admire how nice and tan they are. There's nothing much else to look at—the trees are stick pine and the river is too low and I'd rather be watching Bear on TV instead of listening to my know-it-all boyfriend who'll make something up if he doesn't know the answer. Still, I like to ask him questions. I like the way his voice sounds when he doesn't have a clue.

I point at a big bird, perched at the top of a tree to watch us pass. "Is that a crane?"

"Close," he says. "It's a heron. Cranes fly with their necks out, not pulled back like that. And herons are smaller and have a bimodal toe."

"A what?"

"It's like an opposable thumb."

"Like a person has?"

"Exactly," he says.

When we catch up to Coach's canoe, he throws a leg over so we can float together, pass things back and forth. The psoriasis doesn't look as bad as I thought up close; there are a bunch of red splotches but they look more like razor burn than a lumpy patchwork quilt.

We come to our first stop, a nice spot with a flat rock I like to lay out on.

I lie on my stomach and unhook my top like I don't want to get tan lines, though I don't care about tan lines—I'm pretty enough so that tan lines seem like the kind of flaw that only adds to it.

They watch me while they smoke their joint.

"Have some Doritos," Coach says, tossing a bag next to my head.

I take one and hold it between my teeth while I fix my top. Coach and my boyfriend throw the football and I move to the shallow water and dig my fingers into the mud and gravel—the water between my legs cold and warm and then cold again. I try to catch tiny fish with my hands but they're too fast, so I pluck snails off rocks and drop them back into the water. They make a nice *plunk* sound.

"I forgot my net."

"You can use mine when I'm not using it," my boyfriend says.

"Yours is too big."

"That's what she said!" Coach says.

"You never catch anything anyway," my boyfriend says.

"That's not true. I catch little tiny fishes."

"But then you just let them go."

"I'm not gonna let my fish get eaten by your monster. Throw me the ball." Coach throws it to me but I miss and I give up after that. I want to be able to naturally catch balls or else I don't want to play.

I'm ready to move on to the next spot, but they're having a good time so I open another beer and look closely at rocks and other nothing things, as if it is my job to make something of them. One rock plus one snail plus the tab off my beer can equals what? I wonder where we'll go for dinner. Usually we go to the Chinese buffet but we just had Chinese so we might go to Mexican. I could go back to the Chinese buffet, though. It's better than the Mexican place but I'd probably eat more and I don't want to eat more because I'm getting fat. I measure the roll on my stomach with two fingers but it's just skin. I've seen how these things can happen, though—one day my sister was a stick and the next day a gargantuan.

Eventually my boyfriend says, "I guess we ought to keep moving," and we load up.

Pretty soon, we come to the big fancy house. There's a boy on the balcony and he waves and I wave and it seems like it would be fun up there, a big fancy house overlooking the river.

"Hey," the boy calls down to us, his hands cupping his mouth.

"Hey," I call back. There's nothing to say after that so I lift my paddle into the air and pump it a few times, shaking the water off. The boy is blond, about ten years old. He's been waiting for us—listening to our laughter, our voices carrying over the water.

"Can we live there one day?" I ask my boyfriend, and he

says yes. He always agrees when I ask him things like this—
he'll say *of course* or *okay* and I won't say any more about it,
but he knows I don't really want to live with him in a big fancy
house, that the only way we pull it off at all is by surrounding ourselves with disabled people and drunks, attaching our
lives to the sad, impermanent lives of others.

HE SAYS I AM
A LITTLE OVEN

At The Straw Market, my boyfriend follows a man in a turban, weaving in and out of the aisles until I can no longer see him. His mother and I wait outside, looking at things, considering them. I pick up purses and set them on my shoulder while a woman barks prices. They're purses I wouldn't want at home, but I don't realize this until I get them there, put them in the closet and never take them out.

His mother tries on a wrap. She is short and thick with hair so thin I can see her scalp.

"How do I tie this thing?" she asks, and I set the purse back on the table. We're on a cruise and I'm wearing a pink tank top that says Carnival across the chest, another thing that will be obsolete at home. Her husband is still on the boat, slipping quarters into a slot machine, biding his time until dinner.

I wrap it around her waist and cinch it tightly at the hip. "It looks good. You should buy it," I say, looking around for my boyfriend, who is trying to buy weed. He didn't bring any along because he says drug-and-bomb dogs sniff each bag— once when we get on the boat and once when we get off. I don't know if this is true or not; everything I do is legal. We could each bring two bottles of wine or champagne, which is eight bottles for the two of us because his mother and father don't drink.

I buy two purses, both of them pastel and patterned, knockoffs. I don't even try to talk the woman down. And then I leave his mother and walk into the covered area, down a narrow aisle. There are booths full of every imaginable souvenir and it's too hot and there are too many people. I could slip under a table or behind a curtain and no one would ever find me.

I look at ashtrays and shot glasses, pipes and T-shirts and hats, feeling compelled to touch everything as if I have never before touched glass or cotton or wood.

"Hey," my boyfriend says, grabbing my arm.

We find his mother where we left her and the three of us are walking, cutting wide arcs around the locals trying to sell us things, their services. I watch a young couple haggle with a man and wonder what kind of people get into an unmarked car with a stranger and then I'm thinking about all the times I've done exactly that: the ridiculously hot carpenter in Nashville, hopping onto the back of some guy's motorcycle in Panama City, so many times I could have ended up in a ditch. We stop under a sign with tropical birds on it and his mother asks a man to take a picture of us and one more in case anyone closed their eyes: I tilt my head, part my lips. Then my boyfriend takes a picture of the man and his wife and then a family comes up and we're all laughing and passing our cameras back and forth, thanking each other too many times.

We continue on in the direction of the ship, but I'm not ready to go back—we still have three hours left.

"Let's stop here," I say, as we pass a brightly lit tourist bar.

It's one big room filled with beer signs and sombreros, couples drinking out of tall souvenir glasses. The women are sunburned, wearing dresses that tie around their necks, breasts loose.

His mother orders a bottle of water and my boyfriend doesn't order anything and I order an overpriced rum drink from the specialty menu: the plastic neon-yellow, hourglass-shaped. I wanted to go on an excursion, snorkeling or horseback riding, but my boyfriend doesn't believe in spending money on anything but food and liquor and marijuana and he'll only spend as little as possible on these things, selling marijuana in order to pay for his own, buying the cheapest whiskey available. His body smells like processed meat and fumes. Somehow, impossibly, it is a smell I have grown to love.

I chew my straw between sips and look out the window at the people walking by. Some of them stop and open the door, look around before turning and going back out. There is only so much time before they have to get back on the boat and it must be spent wisely. His mother picks up a menu and we look it over: chicken fingers, hot wings, cheeseburgers.

"It's like Dave & Buster's," I say. "The hot wings come with blue cheese and the chicken fingers come with honey mustard."

"Except there aren't any games and everything's more expensive," my boyfriend says, and I smile because he's paying. I lace my fingers through his and he adjusts our hands; he has ideas about hand-holding.

"I could have another," I say, slurping the ice, but we have wine and champagne on the ship. The champagne is warm but we could ice it down in the sink, which is tiny and silver like in an airplane. Everything is too small except for the bed.

He pays and we walk back, still holding hands, arms swinging. He kisses me on the side of the mouth and it makes me want to have sex with him but his parents are in the cabin next to ours, and we don't have the porn or the egg-shaped vibrator we use at home. I use the vibrator in the morning after he leaves for work and think about having sex with him and it is better than the actual sex, which is confusing—how thinking about a thing can be better than the thing.

We show our IDs and the guy welcomes us back on board. Then we navigate the hallways until we find the right elevator. It's day four and I'm starting to learn my way around; it makes me want to stay longer despite the fact that I get seasick, that we have to eat dinner every night with his parents. We say goodbye to his mother and open the door to our cabin and she opens the door to hers and we hear his parents talking. I know what they're saying without being able to hear: he asks what we did, if we had fun; she asks if he lost any money, how much.

"We should start fucking really hard right now," I say, "like we just couldn't wait."

I jump on the bed and he opens a bottle of red wine, pours us each a plastic cup. I like plastic cups, though. They don't break.

"The headboard banging," I say, rocking back and forth so it knocks gently.

"Stop that," he says.

I pick up the towel shaped like a monkey, a pair of my sunglasses on its face. I fling it open and they go sailing. Every day it is some new towel animal on the bed.

He takes off his shoes, his shirt. I take a sip of my wine and set it on the table. Then I pick it back up and take another sip. I don't like his parents and don't pretend to like them. It is nothing against his parents, in particular.

"What time is it?" I ask.

He looks at his watch. "Four forty-two, there's a clock right there."

"Bingo before dinner. It's so cliché."

"Well," he says, "people like bingo. And you can win a lot of money at bingo."

"I never win anything."

"Everyone says that."

"No, seriously—I've never won anything in my *life*." I think about whether this is true or not and find that it is. "I won a necklace at an auction once but I had to pay for it. It cost me like four dollars."

"You have to tell yourself you're going to win. You have to imagine the money already in your pocket."

"I do that sometimes but when it doesn't work it's even more depressing. I'd rather know I'm going to lose and then, if I ever win, it'll be like a sign or something. It'll signify an important shift."

My boyfriend won this cruise in a slot tournament. He still had to buy our plane tickets, though, and rent a car to get us to the departure point. And then there are the bottles of wine and the drinks in tourist bars and other incidentals like Carnival tank tops, things I want just to see if he will buy them. I look at the letters stretched across my chest, the C already begun to peel, and wonder why I chose pink.

"I guess I better get dressed," I say, taking another sip. I place the cup between my thighs so I don't have to reach any farther than I have to. "Oh—did you find any weed?"

"Shhh," he says, looking at the wall. "I got enough for one joint. I'm going to smoke it tonight."

"What if it's laced?"

"It's not laced," he says.

"How do you know? You bought it from a stranger with a towel on his head."

"A turban. Don't be racist."

"I'm pretty sure it was an actual towel," I say. "When I was in college I had this striped terrycloth dress and I wore it all the time, like I was a kid. I didn't even want to take it off to wash it."

He goes into the bathroom and I pour myself another glass because I'm on vacation, because soon I will have to go to bingo with his parents and eat dinner with his parents and I'll have to smile and be polite, which are things I do anyway but I don't like feeling like they are required. I turn on the TV, which is playing the same movie we watched last night, and then get out of bed and look through the closet. I brought five dresses, one for each night. Before we left, his mother told me I had to wear dresses in the evenings because the dining room is semiformal, but the last cruise she went on was in the early eighties, when cruises and airplanes were still for the well-off.

I choose a low-cut black dress I've had for two years but never worn. Then I sit on the bed and pick up the schedule, check to see what's going on. There is a new schedule every day and I like to read about all of the things I won't do. I like that there are options.

When he comes out, I have him tie my dress in the back, adjust my boobs before turning around.

"Wow," he says. "How come you've never worn this before?"

"Because it's for prostitution and cruising."

"We'll have to take more cruises," he says, squeezing my ass, pressing me into him.

His parents are seated in a booth when we arrive, one of the dancers calling out numbers. I wonder if the dancers share rooms on the bottom level where the workings of the ship keep them up at night. I wonder if they have sex with one another or with the cruisers or if all sex is off-limits and there is a contract about these things. I imagine beautiful young dancers left at various ports of call.

"You look nice," I say, touching his mother's gold bracelet. She's wearing a blue dress with matching shoes and bag. We sit and she tells my boyfriend he has to go up to the stage to pay for the cards and he gets back up and walks to the front.

He has a confident but self-conscious walk: shoulders thrown back and chest out, looking straight ahead but smiling pleasantly like he might stop and chat with somebody at any minute.

His mother pushes her card between us and then a waiter comes and offers us small, free drinks because it's happy hour. We all take one and his mom and dad scoot theirs into the middle of the table. They're nice people, really, but I don't have anything to say to them. His father was in Vietnam, like my father, but he's the kind of veteran who subscribes to a magazine, who saved up the money to go back. My father's brother died in Vietnam and my father hitchhiked across the country to visit him in the hospital but he was already dead. Then he had to go back to war.

"I love this dress," his mother says, and I look at my boobs, which are large and pale and mostly exposed.

"Thanks. It's not something I would wear at home, obviously."

"The weather is supposed to get bad tonight," his father says, smiling.

My boyfriend hands me a bingo card and I wonder where I put my seasick bracelet; it didn't work but it was something— it made my wrist itch and pressed a pattern into it.

"One time I went deep-sea fishing and all the men were throwing up over the sides while I ate lunch," his mother says.

"I was so sick the other night—what night was that— Monday? I just laid in bed and couldn't even watch TV," I say.

"You better not drink too much," my boyfriend says, placing a hand on my knee.

I take another sip of my free drink, cold and electric blue. The next game starts and I mark off the free space. I only get two numbers for a long time and then I get a bunch in a row but they're scattered and somebody yells bingo and waves an arm in the air.

Out of the next four games, my boyfriend wins one and his mother wins one. His mother wins two hundred and fifty dollars and my boyfriend wins blackout for four hundred.

I count his money, hundred-dollar bills, and he takes the bills from me and folds them into his wallet.

"What are you going to buy me?" I ask.

"I don't know, what do you want?"

"A bracelet," I say, touching his mother's wrist. She is round but tiny, her wrist as delicate as a girl's.

"We'll see," he says, patting me like a child.

"There's a jewelry store on board, duty free," his mother says. "I might buy myself a nice watch. I've never had a nice watch." She looks up at her husband, a big man with a full beard and glasses that darken in the sun. She is so small compared to him and for a moment I imagine the two of them having sex, how the arrangement might work.

The dancer announces the six o'clock seating so we file out with most of the audience and then we're all bunched up in a too-small hallway waiting for the doors to open. In this hallway, with all of these people standing too close and talking too loud, I'm reminded what a horrible idea this was, how every night I eat too much and drink too much, how I get seasick.

The waiters fling open the doors and lead us to our seats.

They have accents that are foreign but not so foreign they can't be understood. They form a conga line around the dining room, clapping and singing "Macarena." His mother claps along, bouncing every time her hands meet, and then she leans across the table to ask me what kind of towel animal we got—they got a duck. We got a monkey wearing my sunglasses, I tell her, which makes her ridiculously happy. His father pats his wife's shoulder to the beat and then our waiter stops and takes the salt and pepper shakers off our table for an impromptu juggle. We look like a happy couple, on vacation with his parents. We've been together two years, lived together one.

While we look over our menus, the waiter comes around with a camera.

"Say pigs-in-a-blanket," he says, smiling as if to show us how it's done. "Say money."

When dinner is over, we go back to our room and change. The seas have picked up. It is a gentle rocking that doesn't seem like it should make me sick but it does. I wash my face and brush my teeth and put on the little blue wristband I found in his mother's medicine cabinet; it's old and I'm not sure how it works, or if it's expired. Then I get in bed and stretch out in the middle.

"I can get you some real medicine," he says, brushing the hair out of my face.

"Okay," I say.

"I'll probably smoke my joint first and then go get it."

"Okay," I say again, though I don't like this plan. He'll end up at the dance club talking to girls who take shots out of each other's belly buttons. Girls he calls whores. I turn on the TV and he leaves. It's still the same movie, twenty-four hours of it, but soon another one will start. I check the schedule to see what it is: *Iron Man*. Then I turn off the TV and pick up a book from the table. I bought a whole stack of magazines and two paperbacks at the airport. I bought sushi and expensive coffee and a bag of almonds and now I probably won't have enough money to get me through the rest of the month. I turn on the lamp and try to read but I've had too much to drink, the words blurring on the page. I wonder if I should stick my finger down my throat but I'd probably still feel sick. The upside is that it would get rid of some of the calories I consumed at dinner: four courses ending in a chocolate dish with a crispy top and a warm melty inside. We each had one, scraping our bowls.

I close my eyes and think about the boat on the ocean, black waves and black sky and a sliver of moon, and I like the idea of it—how lonely it looks—but next time I'll just fly wherever I want to go. I'll step out of the airplane onto solid ground.

An hour later, he lets himself in, his eyes bloodshot. They will stay this way for about an hour. He hands me two pills and a cup of water and I sit up and swallow them.

He kisses me, pushes his tongue in my mouth. "My parents are at a show until ten," he says, squeezing my breast. He puts my hand on his dick.

"Baby," I say, "I'm not feeling very well."

"We didn't have sex yesterday or today," he says, "and now we have an opportunity."

I take my hand off him. He likes to have sex twice a day and we've settled on once—a compromise he has made for me. Sometimes he films me and I let him, only my face on camera. On the occasions I refuse to have sex with him, he gets angry and asks me questions that seem to support his position: Am I physically hurting you? Do you enjoy it?

He goes to the bathroom and pees and then tells me he's going to the casino.

"I wish you'd stay with me," I say. "*Iron Man*'s about to start."

"We only have two more nights and I'd like to enjoy them," he says.

"Being with me isn't enjoyable?"

"I didn't say that," he says. "I've seen that movie four times already."

"Stay with me for just a minute."

He sits on the bed and I put my hand on his thigh and then move it to his crotch. He's hard so I stroke him, and then I unzip his shorts and take him in my mouth. He chokes me with it, pushing it to the back of my throat, and I take off my panties because it's easier to just let him fuck me.

I wake up wearing only the wristband and my Carnival tank top. I look around for my panties and find them on the floor: my prettiest pair, lace and bows. He's snoring lightly with his mouth open, his hair so long it has begun to curl itself into loose ringlets. I press myself against him. He doesn't mind if

I lie as close as possible, practically on top of him—he says I am a little oven, that I am good in the winter. I wonder why he doesn't love me anymore, if it's because I'm too strong or too weak. At this point, things have become so muddled that everything feels like an inversion. I say one thing, sure I believe it, and he says the opposite and it sounds right, too, more right than the thing of which I was certain.

I get out of bed and dig through my bag for a pair of shorts, socks, a sports bra. I dress and put a key in my pocket and let myself out, stopping in front of his parents' room to listen: his father coughs; the TV is turned to the news.

I take the stairs up.

The treadmills line the windows so you can look out and see the nose of the boat cutting through the water, dividing it. I stretch and step on, starting slowly and working my way up to a jog. I do it because I like how I look afterwards—cheeks flushed and eyes bright—a look that can't be replicated with makeup. I'm hungover, though, and the water makes me dizzy. I imagine falling off, my body in a heap on the floor, and lose my rhythm.

I run for ten minutes and walk for twenty and take the elevator back down. He's watching *Iron Man* when I come in. "Where'd you go?"

"The gym."

"You weren't gone for very long," he says. "You coming to breakfast?"

People want a good hot breakfast. They want omelets and waffles and eggs and biscuits. They want bacon and sausage.

We're seated at a table with a family of seven. There are five kids, all ugly, of various ages and ethnicities. Each of them is holding something, a shabby animal or a plastic muscle man. I talk to the little girl next to me, a skinny blond with big knees and glasses who has a stuffed kangaroo in her lap. I touch its tail and ask her what his name is.

"*Her* name," she says.

"Okay, *her* name?"

"Jessica."

"Ah," I say, "Jessica." It looks like a dog toy. I unroll the silverware from my napkin and look around for the waiter.

My boyfriend plays his city-councilman role with the father, leaning forward to show interest, looking him directly in the eye. He reads books about this sort of thing. Otherwise, he doesn't read at all. He says he got his master's degree in education without ever reading anything; he just listened and rephrased what others were saying in class. He made all A's doing this.

After we eat, we put on our swimsuits and lay out on the top deck. I walk around in my bikini—fetching towels, getting water—so he can catch men watching me, so he can be proud I am his.

When the waitress comes, I ask him to buy me a drink.

"Okay," he says, "but only one." Maybe he wants to be my father, or he doesn't. He thinks I should learn to stand on my own two feet. I lie back and close my eyes. A moment later, his parents are standing over us, enormous in front of a bright blue sky. It reminds me of the painting classes I took as a kid, how to create the illusion of depth: his father with his round stomach and tinted glasses, his mother with her teased hair and matching outfit. They're almost beautiful from this angle.

"We were looking at the pictures from last night," his mother says. "They're in that big room you walk through to get to the buffet."

"How'd they turn out?" I ask, sitting up on my elbows.

"Y'all look so handsome. You have to buy her one," she says to her son.

"I'll get her one if she wants one."

"Of course she wants one," she says. "How many cruises will y'all take in your lifetime—two, three?" We don't say anything. "Not many," she says. I shield my eyes from the sun and smile up at her.

"We're headed to the buffet," his father says, and we all say goodbye.

"You don't have to buy me a picture. I'm sure we could find something better to do with your fifty dollars."

"You think it costs fifty dollars?" he asks.

"Probably. It's probably one of those blow-up pictures they put in a stupid frame with a boat on it."

"She'll be disappointed if I don't get it for you."

"We can take our own pictures. I have my camera." *A camera you bought for me,* I think, remembering how excited he was for me to unwrap it, something so expensive. Something he hadn't made himself. My drink comes and I drink it fast because taking poor care of myself feels like a sacrifice I am offering him. I set the cup down and turn to look at him. He doesn't acknowledge me so I keep on looking—his upper arms sprouting a few crazy hairs, his second toes longer than the big ones. I want to touch him, want to feel the steady pressure of his hand on mine. I try to remember the last time he said he loved me.

"What'd you do last night?" I ask.

"Went to the casino, lost half the money I won."

"Did you play slots?"

"I don't play slots. My parents play slots."

"Blackjack?"

He lets the question hang there—*blackjack?*—and I think about the drive to Fort Lauderdale, the flight to Atlanta and then the two-hour layover before the flight to Nashville. How long tomorrow will be and then we'll be at his house, our bags full of dirty clothes that won't make it past his kitchen. I reach over and pluck one of the thick, unruly hairs from his arm.

"That hurt. Don't do that again."

I look at the hair attached to a root and let it go. "You're not paying attention to me. Pay attention to me."

"Yes I am—we're tanning together," he says. "Can't you just enjoy yourself for a minute?"

"I *am* enjoying myself," I say, watching a cloud float by. "Will you put some more sunscreen on me?" I pass him the bottle and turn my back to him and he squirts the cool lotion onto my shoulders. It feels nice and he rubs and rubs, trying to get it to soak in. I like to stay as pale as possible, though my shoulders and chest are freckled; as a teenager, I rubbed baby oil all over myself, laid out on sheets of tinfoil. I put lemon juice in my hair and it turned orange.

"I'm going to go to the room and get my camera," I say, putting on my tank top.

And then we're standing at the front of the boat, the wind blowing furiously. I throw my arms out like that scene in *Titanic* and he takes a picture, and I wonder how many people have posed exactly like this—thousands, millions. And for a moment I like the idea of being exactly like everyone else, in my pink Carnival tank top and Old Navy bikini, my knockoff purses. He puts his arm around me and holds the camera up and takes picture after picture, until we are perfectly centered and happy, until he gets it exactly right.

WHERE ALL OF THE
BEAUTIFUL PEOPLE GO

'm on a cheap raft, pink and deflating, trying to keep my body balanced in the center while Aggie sits on a step churning the water. She's high on pills and has recently chopped off all her hair. Her mother has been dead for six days.

I brought cookies from the grocery store, apologizing. I feel bad about the cookies—I should have baked something—though Aggie's family is the kind that prefers Chips Ahoy! to the homemade variety.

"My mother always told me I was too big and clumsy, too much like my father. Mothers are supposed to tell their daughters they're beautiful," she says, and it makes me sad because it's true—it's what all girls most want to hear. I hope I never have a daughter because if I had a daughter and she wasn't beautiful, I'd have to lie and tell her she was and I don't like to lie, not even the nice white ones. Sometimes I think the people who believe they're the most honest are the biggest liars of all. When I start to think this way, nothing makes sense.

"You *are* beautiful. And you're talented. You're so talented."

"Do you think it's bad?" she says. "Do you think I'm a bad person?"

"Of course I don't think you're a bad person. You're in mourning. People do strange things when they're in mourning—they don't think clearly." She doesn't say anything else so I give her a few more variations along these lines, trying to sound as supportive as possible.

When Aggie found out her mother was dying, she applied for credit cards in her mother's name. She received a number of them with limits from three hundred dollars to three thousand. I can imagine some of the stuff she ordered off the TV—charm bracelets and clothes that don't wrinkle, gimmicks to help you cook breakfast foods more efficiently. She purchased a new set of living room furniture, which should arrive any day now. Maybe today. She's very excited about this new furniture; she has never had a whole matching set before. I don't care about things like this so it's hard for me to understand, but I also don't have a husband or a house or kids. Maybe if you get a husband and a house and kids you automatically want a nice set of matching furniture so badly you're willing to steal for it.

I wish I had a dog. I think about dogs a lot. In the past month, I've been to the pound five or six times, but I can't make a decision; I don't trust my judgment. They don't even call it the pound anymore. My sister says I only like the neurotic ones, the ones that will only love me, that will snarl and nip at the heels of anyone who isn't me. But I also think: *What's so wrong with that?*

Sometimes I call to ask if the dog I like is still there. *Is Gunner still available?* I ask, and then wait a long time for someone to check and a few times they said no, he was adopted, and one time a woman—she must have been new—told me the dog had been exterminated. Exterminated! But usually the dog is still there and I tell them I'll be by in the morning but morning comes and I stay in bed and think about dogs, how a dog would get me up and outside, how a dog would look at me with its worshipful eyes and make me feel guilty for not being the person I know I could be.

If I wanted a dog at this point, I don't even think they'd give me one. They know me there, though I try to disguise myself. Some days I'm dressed up, wearing a skirt and high heels; other days I'm two days' dirty in workout clothes.

"I really want that furniture," Aggie says, "and I can't send it back now." She tells me all about it—how many pieces, the color and fabric—but I don't listen. I take a sip of my beer and wonder how many more her husband has in the refrigerator and whether he'd notice if I drank them all. Aggie doesn't drink because she takes too many pills but I never see her take them. It makes me wish I had some other, less obvious vice.

Her husband opens the door and their sons tumble outside. He holds my gaze and then watches me for a moment from behind the glass. He's friendly, smiling and hospitable, which contradicts everything Aggie tells me about him so I see him as a menacing figure. He was a cop but now he isn't. Now he does something with computers. His name is George. My mother and her sister used to call their periods "George" because they hated the name—"George is here," they'd say, groaning, or as an explanation for why they needed to stay in bed: "George came late last night," but then her sister married a man named George and they'd had to stop.

The younger boy is carrying the bag of wedding cookies I brought so I paddle over and open it for him. He starts shoveling them into his mouth. I loved wedding cookies growing up, the powdered sugar on my fingers, a delicate sprinkling on my shirt.

"Hop on, Bucko."

"My name's not Bucko!"

His name is Nathan. Nateybear, I call him, Natekabob. Cowboy. Superhero. Trashman. Beetlejuice. Peewee. Ghostrider. Angelhead. He screams every time because he loves it, or maybe he doesn't. I don't know. It's about the only way I can get him to say anything. He climbs onto the raft, further deflating the situation, and straddles me. I use my arms to paddle us back to the middle of the pool where it feels more private.

Nathan has blue eyes that droop down at the corners. They make him look sad and wise and I like him much better than the other one, Alexander, who's a few years older and looks like a picture of a boy in a book—plain and perhaps more conventionally attractive, but dull. It won't be long before people start introducing themselves to him again and again and he knows what it's like to be completely forgettable.

I run my fingers through Nathan's hair, slick it back, and then press his cheeks together until his lips are tiny and fishlike. He pinches me on the side, just below my bikini top; it's the last place I lose weight and the first place I gain. I slap his hand and he readjusts.

Aggie doesn't give him enough attention—he is starved for physical contact—because she spends a lot of time in bed with migraines or vertigo or whatever she's calling it. Depression, I want to say, just call it what it is, but I don't want to say it, either. I call mine insomnia, stomach issues. Perhaps a simple gluten or lactose intolerance, something easily fixed with a change in diet or a hot bath followed by a cool room and clean sheets.

I push Nathan off and he goes under. When he surfaces, he paddles back to me, grabs onto my raft, and we're capsizing.

"It's all over!" I yell. "Goodbye, so long!" And then we're both in the water and he's flinging his chubby arms around my neck—I love how they crease at the elbow—and wrapping his legs around my waist. I want this boy. Aggie doesn't deserve him. He's probably never been to the circus or an amusement park or the beach. I bet he hasn't even been to a zoo, though I wouldn't take him to a zoo, or I'd take him to one and explain why zoos are bad and why all of the animals should be living in their natural habitats unless they're about to go extinct or would immediately die in the wild. I'd tell him about Inky the Octopus, who broke out of his tank in the middle of the night, slid down a six-inch-wide drainpipe and back out into the Pacific Ocean, leaving a trail of suction cup marks in his wake.

"Would you return it?" Aggie asks.

"What? I thought we'd settled this already."

"I just want to know if you'd give it back."

I swim over to her. Her eyes don't look right. They don't look right at all. "I don't know. I guess I wouldn't have done it—I do a lot of awful things but stealing's not one of them." I notice a long dark hair on my chest. I try to pull it out but it just curls. Now that I've seen it, I can't stop looking at it.

"It's not stealing," she says. "We applied for them and they gave them to us."

"You applied for one the day she died."

"It was the day before, and I didn't know she was going to die. I haven't even used that one yet."

"I take magazines, actually. At the gym, at doctor's offices, everywhere but the store, so I guess I *do* steal, though I don't really think of it as stealing because I usually leave one behind like a leave-one-take-one situation, though there's nothing that says it's a leave-one-take-one situation so I guess it's just plain stealing. And sometimes I don't have one to leave behind."

"See?" she says, churning the water more forcefully. "We all steal something."

"Okay, so here's what you're going to do—you're going to keep all of the furniture and everything else and not feel bad about it. And then you're going to cut the cards up. If you start returning stuff it might look suspicious."

"I didn't think about that," she says, "but you're right. I better not return anything."

"Now stop thinking about it. I give you permission to stop thinking about it."

Her arms go still but the waves keep coming.

Aggie gives me pills; this is why I'm friends with her. Otherwise, I wouldn't drive all the way to Round Rock to swim in her pool. My apartment complex has its own pool where I swim laps back and forth and help the maintenance man with small jobs. "Will you take the hose out in half an hour?" he might ask, and I am happy to be given such a reasonable and achievable task. For the most part, I hoard the pills because I like having them, same as I like having extra toilet paper and a pantry full of nonperishable food items. I collect pill cases and put them in there all blue and white and yellow and they're so pretty. She passes them across the table to me in restaurants—The Cheesecake Factory, Chili's, cavernous Mexican places with half-price margaritas—like they're Tylenol or loose change. Sometimes she gives me an entire bottle and I just stick it in my purse and try not to look around, but then I do. I can't help it. I look around and people look at me because I'm looking at them and one time I dropped the bottle and it rolled into someone's foot.

My boyfriend would break up with me if he knew, if he found them hidden in the suitcase where I keep my illicit things. He doesn't do drugs or smoke cigarettes and only drinks in moderation. This morning he got angry with me about the way I squeeze my toothpaste. I don't squeeze it right, from the bottom up. He isn't the first one to mention it but it seems to bother him more than the others and I wonder why it's so important. It's just toothpaste. Luckily he lives out of town and I don't see him that often. Ten minutes after he left, I was on my way to Round Rock, stopping at the grocery store to pee and pick up cookies before getting lost in Aggie's neighborhood, which looks like all of the surrounding neighborhoods, and then parking in front of her house that looks like all of the other houses, everything beige and neat and treeless. The curtains closed. This is the place you move if you really want to disappear.

I climb back onto the raft—it is getting to be a desperate situation. I need another beer but I don't want to get out and dry myself off and make my way into the kitchen, encountering Aggie's husband on the couch, which seems perfectly nice enough, just like a couch. I imagine standing before the enormous TV, baseball or golf, and watching with him for a moment to be polite. But a few minutes later he comes out and asks if the ladies need anything.

"Will you get me another? Do you mind that I'm drinking all your beer?"

He doesn't mind. I smile and row myself over, set my empty down and wait.

"It's Coors," George says, as if I can't see that it's Coors. He removes my huggie from the empty can and puts it on the fresh one. "We're out of Heineken."

"This is great. Perfect."

"Holler if you need another."

I thank him and push off. George doesn't know about the credit cards. He would kill her, she says, or beat her to a pulp. But where does he think the money's coming from? Perhaps she told him her mother had cashed in a policy or had an emergency savings account they didn't know about. Perhaps he trusts her.

George is older than Aggie by ten years, his hair gray and

bushy, and Aggie is older than me by another ten, or twelve. He must wonder why I'm friends with his wife. I can't look at him without thinking about the things I know that he doesn't know—that she steals—not just this credit card scam but from stores, too. She gets away with it, she says, because she doesn't look the type; frequently, she's with her children. And she contacts men over the internet and goes over to their houses or meets them in motel rooms because George can't get it up anymore. I've told her that this is insanely dangerous and irresponsible, but I like hearing about these men.

Aggie is a storyteller, describing the situations in great detail: how they feel the need to explain themselves, how she goes through their things when they're in the bathroom or taking a shower. They leave their wallets on the counter, along with their keys. She could take anything, and she does, though she carefully considers whether it is something that might be noticed. She shows me these tokens—voter ID cards and movie stubs and matches—spread out on her bed when we lock the door from George and the children. They remind me of the souvenirs of serial killers.

Mostly I'm surprised that they go through with it, every time. Never has a man taken a look at her and backed out. Never has Aggie driven somewhere, parked, and decided against it, opting instead for a cheeseburger and a milkshake.

There was an accident years ago. I know the basics: a car crash; someone died. She was in a coma for a long time and they didn't think she'd come out of it and then she did. I didn't know her before the accident but it's clear she's not the person she would have been. There are her eyes, for one, which aren't like regular eyes. And there is the way her brain works, which is not like a regular brain, and there are all of the pills, which she began taking in order to cope.

I had a friend once who was divorcing her husband because she despised him and then she had a seizure and forgot that she despised him and called the divorce off. Her husband was still the same guy he'd always been but her brain had been reset to the time she'd met him, back when he was her one and only, when she couldn't remember all of the things that had happened in between falling love and filing for divorce.

When I think of the Aggie I know and the Aggie I might have known, I think of this friend I'm no longer friends with and whether I would still be friends with her if she hadn't had the seizure.

Alexander screams because he sees a salamander. He loves the baby salamander. He gets down on all fours to look at it and then Nathan scrambles out of the pool and kneels beside him and they give us updates about its movement. They wonder where his family is and if he's lost, if he's sad. Alexander asks if they should kill him, if they should put him out of his misery, and this makes me reconsider Alexander and my blanket dismissal of him.

Aggie takes hold of my raft, pushing me back and forth in a lulling, pleasant motion.

"Want me to blow it back up for you?" she asks.

"Maybe in a minute. Thanks."

I wonder what they'll have for dinner, if they'll invite me to stay. This past Thanksgiving, I couldn't fly home so I ate with them here. Everything had come from a box or a can and I met her mother and her mother's husband and her brother and his family and they were all wearing pleated blue jeans and sweatshirts with various designs and decorations and I had loved the whole affair—the blandness and mediocrity of it—and how they'd had no idea it was bland or mediocre. Tombstone pizza, perhaps, or frozen meatballs boiled in Ragú. Bunny bread on a plate, potatoes made from flakes, half of a pound cake in half of a plastic box.

She stops pushing and I touch her hand; the pushing resumes. She tells me she's doing the best she can, that she does the best she can.

"I know," I say. "We all do." I close my eyes and think about this. I could do better, it's completely within my ability, and Aggie could do better, but we allow ourselves to neglect the most important things as we tell ourselves we're doing our best. I open my mouth and close it, decide to keep this information to myself. I think I might fall asleep but then I hear thunder in the distance and remember the place I lived before moving to Austin, how those two years were full of storms and I'd stop whatever I was doing to go out to my balcony and watch them. When the parking lot flooded, the cars would pause before the water. Sometimes they reversed and turned around but mostly they just plowed right through.

"My counselor says I have low self-esteem," I say, perhaps as a way of evening things out.

"I'm sorry," she says. She seems really sorry, like this is terrible news.

"I think I'm going to stop seeing her—I spend most of my

time thinking about *her* life. And there's nothing really wrong with my life. My life is perfectly fine."

Aggie is nearly unresponsive but she keeps pushing and I keep talking about my counselor and her shoe collection and how she doesn't wear a wedding ring but maybe she takes it off before sessions? On my worst days, the only way I can get through the fifty minutes is by imagining her alone in a dark apartment drinking vodka martinis. And then I start telling her about my boyfriend and how glad I am he doesn't live here, how he wants me to be someone else even though he liked me fine at the beginning. Loved me, even, just the way I was, and this is how it always goes. I end my soliloquy with, "Men, you can't live with 'em."

This stirs something in her. "Aren't you forgetting the second half?"

"No," I say. "That's the end of it."

"Men," she says, "you can't live with 'em and you can't live without 'em."

"I know the saying."

When the furniture comes, Aggie is sharp, sober. She wraps a towel around her waist and hurries inside. Alexander follows and it's just Nathan and me. He tries to climb onto my raft and I let him struggle before helping him. He gestures toward the cookies and we paddle over.

"Give me one," I say, opening my mouth wide. He drops a cookie in. "These were my favorite when I was a kid."

"You weren't a kid," he says, and he laughs and laughs.

I tell him he's had enough, that he's going to get diabetes. I don't know if I could give him a better life but I could wean him off sugared cereal and Chef Boyardee and take him to Whole Foods so he could see where all of the beautiful people go. He paws at my breasts with his pruned fingers. How old is he? I have difficulty with the years between three and six.

I grab his hands and he leans forward and kisses me full on the mouth.

"You can't French kiss me," I say. "It's disgusting. It's not right!" I wipe my mouth in an exaggerated manner as he squeals and think of the time I saw a dog and a pig playing together on the side of the road, how happy it had made me. Then I think of Gunner and Biscuit, Echo and Willy and Winter, all of the dogs I might have had if I'd played my cards right. Gunner was my favorite—snow white with black rings around his eyes. When I walked him up and down the driveway, he didn't pull at the leash but stayed right by my side, occasionally looking up at me to wag his tail, no doubt in his mind that all of his troubles were in the past, already forgotten.

LOVE APPLES

He tells you a story about women who put peeled apples under their arms, how they would send these apples off to war with their men and the men would eat them, so what he is requesting is not so much.

He wants you to send him a sweaty T-shirt, or some panties you got excited in.

That night you sleep under a heavy comforter. In the morning you take off your shirt and wrap it up in a piece of tissue paper. It is thin and worn and ocean blue. You picture it draped across his chest.

The post office is empty, the bald guy reading the newspaper.

"Nice and quiet in here," you say, because even though you are getting a divorce and starting a new life with a man who wants your dirty panties it is no reason to be impolite.

"Twenty people lined up a minute ago," he says, folding. You hand him the envelope and tell him to send it the cheapest way possible. Then you ask about mail forwarding and he gives you a request form with the stipulation that you are to tell everyone you know. "Don't count on us," he says, pointing to himself.

"Through wind and rain."

He smiles as he wags his finger. You tell him you bet he never heard that one before, as if knowing you are the same as everyone somehow makes it better, and he winks and you gather your things and walk out into the too-bright day.

While your husband is at work, you talk to your boyfriend. You met your boyfriend online, in a chat room for people who are interested in films but no one ever talked about films. They talked about fucking; they talked about their wives and husbands and how badly they had been mistreated so they wouldn't feel so badly about talking about fucking.

You get to know each other over the phone, over drinks, in the middle of the day. He works from home and you haven't had a job since the last time you got sick, conjuring up an illness that existed only in your head, which promptly went into remission with your two weeks' notice.

"Are you online?" he asks. Of course you're online, so he sends you a photo of penises in a lineup: small, small-average, average, large-average, large. His is large-average. He wants to give you an idea. You tell him you're reading a novel that takes place inside a woman's head, during the span of a blow job.

At five o'clock, you stand at the door with the phone pressed to your ear and watch out the peephole. The peephole is your height, installed by your husband so you wouldn't have to answer the door for anyone you didn't want to answer

the door for, and now the only people who come to the door
are people you're certain you don't want to talk to. Your social
life is limited to the old lady across the street. When your car
is in the driveway, you're home, so she calls and you go over
to her house and drink a flat Coke and try to come up with
a reason to leave, or you watch Sunday services with her in
the back room and she points out people in the congregation,
tells you the things they have done and the things that have
been done to them and you say how terrible it all is.

Your boyfriend is saying he has waited an eternity.

Now he is saying he will take you to Korea, Japan, India,
Iceland. The world is so big and you have seen so little of it.
All of the people you used to know are strangers but if you
saw one of them on the opposite side of it then maybe you
could say hello. "I'm hungry," you say. "Eat an apple," he says,
but you don't feel like eating an apple. When the two of you
are together you won't want to eat pizza anymore. You won't
want to eat sandwich cookies. Where is your husband? He
said he'd take you to The Hungry Heifer, where the wait-
resses wear T-shirts with cows on the back of them, because
you asked, because he is a nice guy even though you are leaving and he will probably die without you. Whose back will
he scratch? Who will watch Cops with him? You don't think
about these things, and you don't think about how quiet the
house will be, how he will lie in bed and listen to your absence.

He pulls up in his little white truck and gets out and you
watch him get bigger and bigger. You tell your boyfriend you
love him terribly, goodbye. Soon you will have a new life.

You will be in love. You *are* in love. You are also drunk. Your husband's head is so big when viewed through the peephole. You unlock the door as he is unlocking the door and he steps inside. He has a case of beer even though it's Tuesday.

"I have to go bad," you say, and you turn and run to the bathroom and pee with the door open. *You've sprung a leak!* your husband usually says, but he doesn't say it today so you say it quietly to yourself. You spread your legs and watch one fast stream split into two and then three and then you take a handful of stomach and pinch. Your boyfriend has no idea how big you are. You are going to lose the weight before you meet him.

"Are we going to the Heifer?" you ask.

Your husband kneels in front of the refrigerator with the box. He places the cans in the drawer and then he stands and leans against the counter. His earplugs hang around his neck, yellow and squishy. The plant he works at is loud. He has to wear a hard hat in certain areas and steel-toed boots. He has a small office where he spends his days, avoiding the chatty secretary and the corporate people who pass through. The Bigwigs, he calls them. If they catch him they make him go to fish camp and eat at a round table and he doesn't like to be looked at while he's eating. You don't like to be looked at while you're eating, either.

He doesn't feel like going out. Plus it's too expensive, and the portions too small—this has never bothered him before. He clomps down to the basement with a can of beer. The cigarette smoke seeps into the house. You hear the garage door open so you move to the window and watch him step from one patch of grass to the other like he is trying to stamp them out. It's about the saddest thing you ever saw but you back away from the window and sit on the couch with your laptop on your lap and double click on the Firefox icon, noticing for the first time that the fox is wrapped around a globe, and remind yourself that you are in love. You are going to have a life with a man who will take you all over the world whereas your husband doesn't like to cross state lines even though you can't even see them.

Up and down and up and down, cold beer, cold beer.

After a while, he comes back up and sits to watch you shred important documents, the kind he would keep. But they are yours and you are shredding them.

"You don't even know this guy," he says.

You pick up a strip of paper and there is your Social Security number, completely intact. He rolls the chair around to face you—legs spread, swiveling. You don't know what to say. You only know that you are dying but you don't say this because he would say you were being dramatic, he would say you are fine, that everything is fine, because there is nothing left for him to do but insist.

He is hungry. Now you have sobered up and he's drunk so you drive him to Taco Bell. At the drive-thru he tells you he wants a Mexican Pizza and you tell the man you want a Mexican Pizza. Your husband leans forward to look at the menu. The man says, "Is that all?"

"And a Fiesta Burrito," your husband says.

"And a Fiesta Burrito," you say.

"And a Meximelt," he says, sitting back to signal the end of his order.

"And a Meximelt," you say, and then you decide that you might like a Meximelt, too, so you order another Meximelt and tack on a bean burrito and the man tells you to drive around to the second window without giving you your total.

At home, your husband opens his Mexican Pizza and all the cheese has been transferred to the top of the box. He is upset about this. He is more upset about this than he is about your leaving. He takes pictures to document the situation, saying he will send them to the manager and they will send him coupons for free bean burritos, which are your favorite. Of course he will give them to you. Why does he have to be so nice? You could kill him. The two of you sit side by side on the couch and eat too much and watch television and it's just like any other night except that it will all be over soon.

At nine o'clock, he hands you the remote and goes into the bedroom and shuts the door. You don't even wait for him to fall asleep before you call your boyfriend. Your boyfriend says this shows loyalty, the fact that you will not sleep in the bed with your husband anymore. I'm an awful person, you tell him, but he doesn't believe you.

The next day the old lady calls and you tell her you have a roast in the oven but she pretends she can't hear you so you tell her you'll be right over.

You stand at the edge of your driveway looking at a bunch of mushrooms that sprung up overnight. You nudge a big one and it leans over. Then you step on a couple of smaller ones, enjoying the crush of them under your flip-flops. The rest you leave for later.

Her front door is open a crack. You say hello and step inside.

She's wearing a housedress that exposes every bone in her chest. You could ball her up like a piece of construction paper. Her maid asks if you want anything to drink and you say a Coke please and thank you and thank you again when she delivers it, your politeness so polite it is condescending even though you don't mean for it to be condescending. You only mean to be polite.

The two of you sit on either side of the window, where you look out at your street.

"The Mexicans are moving in," she says.

"There must be a dozen in the green house on the corner," you tell her, but you don't care if the Mexicans are moving in, or the blacks, or the polka-dotted people, as your mother used to say when she wanted to demonstrate her sense of equality—*they could be polka-dotted for all I care.* Just then the Mexicans' dog ambles past, jauntily. He's a yellow Lab and there's nothing remotely Mexican about him but he's always loose, unleashed. On the small table between you, your glass sits on a coaster. Next to your glass is her checkbook. The old lady is rich, you are sure, though her house is always hot and her Coke always flat and the only baked goods come in plastic grocery store containers. You wonder if she will leave you any money. You know she won't but you like the idea of it. She has no one and you have no one, but this isn't true. You have a lot of people. You run down the list of them in your head: a mother and a father and a brother and a sister and a husband and a boyfriend and at least four friends you could call up and pour your heart out to, but what would they say? They are always running late. She will leave her money to First Baptist, or to the university where her son taught. Maybe it will be enough to buy him a wing.

You finish your drink and tell her you have laundry in the dryer but her hearing goes out again so you sit there fingering the tablecloth. She asks if you like it and you say it's pretty and she says she'll teach you to crochet but her hands are gnarled. She holds them like a pair of socks. You look at her grandson's senior portrait on the wall—gorgeous and long-haired, eighteen years old—and wish you'd known him then, in the backseat of a Buick, perhaps: his hands on your thighs, your breasts, his teeth on your neck. Now he's in his fifties and chews with his mouth open, food falling out. Not even his eyes give it away.

You stand at a window that is halfway open, watching an assortment of middle-aged women drink coffee and flip through a picture album and talk on the phone about car repairs and birthday parties. No one looks up. They all want to see who will give up first. Your husband stands beside you. You look at him: you will never have his baby and that baby will never have his eyelashes or his thick, wavy hair.

You say something—you have to go to the bathroom, you're thirsty, will these bitches ever shut up?—and he's angry because you ate garlic. He backs away and you put a hand to your mouth and the lady with the picture album walks over and asks how she can help and he hands her the paperwork he filled out at the dining room table, calling you over every few minutes to sign your name as if he were doing the taxes.

On the way home, he pulls into the parking lot of Quiznos and you go inside and order while he waits in the car. He doesn't have to tell you what he wants because you know what he wants. You have no idea what your boyfriend would want. He could order the tuna and you wouldn't be surprised.

There's a line of people in business clothes to remind you it is Thursday. Every day people get up and go to work whereas every day you are relieved to see another blank square on the calendar you got free at the Indian takeout.

The stocky guy with the beard says, "What, no cookie?" and you say, "Not today," and he smiles as he shoves a wad of napkins in your bag, but other days he acts like he's never seen you before in his life.

Your boyfriend reads books and watches videos on how to pleasure a woman, how to make her squirt. You don't squirt, nor do you have any desire to squirt. You can barely change the sheets as it is. But your boyfriend wants to make you squirt because no one else has. He sends you a link to a video, which you watch together: a woman lies on her back on a table and a professional-looking man puts two fingers inside her and begins jerking up hard. "It doesn't hurt," your boyfriend says. "It just looks like it hurts." The man on the screen is explaining the mechanics as if he were taking apart a toaster and then the woman goes into convulsions and a liquid pours out of her. "Disgusting," you say, but you get him off the phone quick.

Your parents come on Saturday with a U-Haul and you load it up with heavy bookcases and china and—since you are the one leaving—all of the wedding pictures and videos and whatever other burdens that will fit. The last thing you take off the wall is the framed photograph of yourself as a child: curly hair and a pink crocheted poncho, an oversized Raggedy Ann doll in the chair next to you. He loves the picture because you look foreign—you are his little foreign poncho girl. You ask if he wants to keep it and he turns around and walks into the kitchen.

Your father doesn't know what's going on, only that you are unhappy, which he doesn't consider reason enough for anything.

Your mother knows there is someone else. Crazy sex brain, she calls it.

You follow behind them in your car, singing along to Sheryl Crow, who writes soundtracks for this sort of thing. You are free, you tell yourself. You are in love. You put your sunglasses on and crack the sunroof so you can hear the truckers blow their horns at you as you pass.

Outside Birmingham, your father pulls the U-Haul into Wendy's. You emerge sweaty and rumpled. You lift your arm and sniff and then run your fingers over your scalp, which is bumpy like a topographical map. You looked it up on the internet and determined that it was psoriasis: an immune disorder resulting in the overproduction of skin cells. Regular skin is on a thirty-day cycle whereas your skin is replacing itself every three or four days, intent upon starting over. It is a disease. There are support groups for it. Other than Brownies, you've never belonged to anything and you like the idea of having supporters, a group of people who sit around in a circle and drink coffee and maybe have sex with each other afterwards.

You tell your father you want a grilled chicken sandwich with no honey mustard and a Diet Coke and go to the bathroom while they wait in line. You look at yourself in the mirror. You feel sorry for yourself like you feel sorry for pretty girls in wheelchairs, like you felt sorry for your friend Angela's dad, who was so big he never left the house.

When you come out, your mother and father are seated by the window.

"I got you the combo," your father says. You did not want the combo. If you had wanted the combo you would have asked for the combo.

The plan is for you to live with your parents until your divorce is final, until your boyfriend can save up enough money to rescue you, until you lose the weight. You see now this plan has holes.

You stuff the fries into your mouth one at a time without swallowing until your mouth is full of potato and think of all the times you've tried to lose the weight—how you would get on the scale to find you'd lost a few pounds and then, pleased with yourself, eat your way back up to where you started.

. . .

At your parents' house, your father makes three drinks, vodka over ice with lime and a splash of tonic, and then goes outside to smoke cheap cigars.

"When did this start?" you ask your mother.

"It's been a while," she says, and she tells you that she smuggled him a box of Cubans when she went to Grand Cayman but he doesn't like the Cubans. Your mother is a compact woman of sixty. You can't imagine her smuggling anything, nor can you imagine that she might get in trouble for doing so.

Your father comes back in and pours another round of drinks and then there is the inevitable talk of pizza. You want a pizza but you don't want to be responsible for the arrival of a pizza.

"What do you think?" your father asks, and they turn and look at you.

"We'll order the thin crust," your mother says.

"Thin crust veggie?"

"Thin crust meat-fest," your father says. "I can't eat no fucking rabbit food." He looks at you and grins. This is also new, his use of four-letter words.

"We'll order you a veggie and your father a meat lover's," your mother says. She goes to the phone and the little dog comes over and sits on your lap. Pot-licker, your father calls her, dump truck. You pet her heavily, rougher than you should but she doesn't seem to mind. If you had a baby, you might manhandle it. You might make it cry and feel terrible. No you wouldn't, of course you wouldn't. You'd love it more than anything. You would die for it, probably. The world news comes on. You don't pay attention but the noise is comforting, like your parents' house is comforting, like regression is comforting before the hole opens up and turns you inside out. You can always go home, you tell yourself. You can always get in your car and go home.

You go upstairs and call your boyfriend. He tells you he sold his truck to a friend for two hundred dollars. It was worth at least a grand but it wouldn't have made it all the way to Tennessee and his friend needed a car. In California, apparently, this is how people operate. You take off your clothes and lie in bed. You get under the covers and listen as he reads you a story but you lose interest and then you fall asleep and dream you're in San Francisco, riding on his handlebars as he bikes around the city and you are thin and beautiful and balance easily but you wake up because you have to pee and can't go back to sleep because you are excited about your new life even though there is nothing to be excited about, as far as you can tell, at least not immediately.

HAMILTON POOL

Darcie hasn't seen rain in over a year. She looks out the window, watches for signs. In the mornings, it's cloudy. At night, there's a breeze. These things don't mean anything anymore but she tracks them regardless.

This morning it is unusually cloudy. She sits on the couch drinking coffee while Terry boils eggs. Downstairs, the baby begins to cry; somebody is moving something or bumps into a wall. Their apartment is on the second floor of a house, a married couple with a baby below—the man an architect, the woman a lawyer. The baby is often strapped to the chest of the woman, who goes about her business as if he isn't there.

Darcie watches the fat-bodied quail pick through the dirt and gutted-out pecans. They make a lot of racket. The birds here are loud and insistent and have different calls than the birds back home because they're different birds. It makes her feel lonely to think about it—her mother and father having drinks together in the living room, talking about the dogs and what they're going to have for dinner. She wonders if they talk about her, or her sister, Laurie. She wonders if they'll ever meet her boyfriend, but she knows they wouldn't like him because he's covered in tattoos, because he was in prison.

Terry hands her a bowl with two eggs rolling around. "Do you want salt?" he asks.

"Yes, please." He brings her the salt, a paper towel. "Where are your eggs?"

"I ate them already. I'm going to heat up some tortillas. Do you want one?"

"Are they stale?" she asks.

"I don't think so. When did we buy them?"

"I don't remember."

"I think it was Tuesday," he says. "What did we do Tuesday?"

"I don't know," she says. "I don't remember Tuesday." He goes back to the kitchen, which is the only place she can't see him from the couch, and she picks up an egg and knocks it against the bowl. The eggs are brown and spotted and come from the next-door neighbor's chickens. Their shells are more fragile than the bleached eggs she used to buy at the store: you set them on the counter and they break; you squeeze them in one hand and they bust. She'd always heard you couldn't break an egg this way.

Terry hands her a tortilla and then sits on his side of the couch and eats, looks out the window. She thinks about her last boyfriend, how he was always so eager to go out. This boyfriend isn't like that. He'll sit around with her all day. He says he'll never cheat on her and it's easy to believe him because they're hardly ever apart.

"It looks like rain," he says.

"It's not going to rain," she says, rolling the tortilla up. It has bits of jalapeño in it, her favorite. "It's just fucking with us."

"It, what?"

"The clouds," she says. "Nature. God."

He puts his thick fingers in her hair and yanks through to the ends. Then he goes over to the bookshelf and sorts through the DVDs. The DVD collection is something from their past life, when he worked fifty hours a week, building things. This wasn't that long ago—three months, four—when they went to the bar at night and picked up a new movie every time they were at Target, when they'd go to Saturday afternoon bar-beques so high they could hardly speak. They bought other stuff, too: a juicer, thick bath towels and camping equipment, a couch big enough for the two of them.

"Have you seen *The Box*?" he asks.

"No. Have you?"

"Part of it," he says, "not the beginning." He puts it in. "It's pretty weird. Be prepared." He takes the cushions off the back of the couch to make more room, and then climbs over her and organizes their bodies, their pillows and blankets. She looks at him and feels happy, but the happiness is heavy, like something should be done with it.

One day, he's going to make her his wife, he tells her. They'll have a little boy and a little girl and a house set back from the street. They'll have their own chickens. Sometimes she doesn't feel like pretending and asks how he's going to support two kids when he can't afford to take her out to dinner, but it's more fun to imagine his blue eyes and long lashes on their babies.

Onscreen, Cameron Diaz and her husband sit in their kitchen looking at the box—taking it apart, unlocking it with the key and locking it again. If they push the button, someone will die, someone they don't know, and they'll receive a suitcase containing one million dollars.

"Would you push the button?" she asks.

"*Hell* no," he says, like is she crazy?, but he's seen what happens after the button has been pushed. She knows it can't be anything good because that wouldn't make for a very interesting movie but she doesn't know the particulars.

"I think I might push the button," she says. "People die all the time. People are constantly dropping dead." She presses her nose to his shoulder and breathes in alcohol and sun-dried tobacco, and under that, the smell of him. She's read about the science of smell, how people are attracted to those who have divergent immunity patterns. They would pass along a wide range of immunities to their children.

"Would you leave me if I pushed the button?" she asks.

"No," he says, shaking her arm, which means she should be quiet now.

He falls asleep holding onto her leg, occasionally stirring enough to kiss her back, as she becomes more and more bored. When it's finally over, he gets up and goes over to the bookshelf. "There's nothing here I want to see," he says. He takes off his shirt, his round belly hard. She keeps waiting for him to lose weight but he doesn't seem to have lost a single pound; no matter how little money there is, there is always plenty to eat.

"How many condoms do we have left?" she asks, though

she knows there is one condom. There are five cigarettes and two Four Lokos and one flask of whiskey above the stove that they don't touch. They're saving it. They'll know what they are saving it for when the time comes.

"One, for tonight." He turns and winks and then goes back to the DVDs. "We'll have to go to campus and swipe some."

"I could get back on the pill," she says, but he knows she doesn't want to get back on the pill. The pill makes her crazy.

He mutes the television and resumes his place on the couch, closes his eyes.

"Don't go to sleep," she says, and it's her turn to shake his arm. He opens his eyes and kisses her and closes them again. She traces his tattoos with her fingers: the Mayan totem pole on his arm, three crazed jokers on his chest, his last name in ornate letters in a half-circle above his belly button. She fingers one of the large black stars on his stomach. In prison, he was a captain in an Aryan gang but that was a long time ago and prison isn't like the outside world. In prison, you have to pick a team based on the most obvious thing and stick with it.

"I wish you hadn't gotten all these racist tattoos," she says.

"I wish I hadn't gotten them either," he says. The dragons on his arms cover up the words WHITE PRIDE. The stars cover up swastikas. The wings on his back—she forgets what these are covering up. She wouldn't mind having wings but she doesn't have any tattoos and if she got them now she would only be reminded she was late, that she had missed something.

"There you are," he says. He puts his finger on the naked

lady on the inside of his left arm. The naked lady has the usual cartoon body: large breasts, a tiny waist, and full hips. Long wavy hair down to her ass. "You had longer hair then."

"That's not me," Darcie says. "I never had hair like that."

She thinks about the questions she used to ask him, how his answers were technically true and yet not true at all. For example, she asked if he ever stabbed anyone and he said he didn't. Later, he told her he didn't stab anyone because a knife wasn't as efficient as bringing a rock down hard on somebody's head. She asked if he killed anyone and he said he didn't but then he told her he assigned people to carry out hits—the orders would come down from above and he was responsible for making sure they were carried out. That person was going to die, regardless, he explained. They were bad people, people who deserved to die. Darcie spent months asking the wrong questions and now she doesn't ask questions and he tells her all sorts of things, more than she wants to know. She lets him talk because she wants to understand him—how he divides things into good and bad, how he believes the bad things he has done are actually good—but no matter how he explains them, she doesn't understand.

She presses her lips to his and he opens his mouth, using a lot of tongue like she likes, and she gives him the soft moans he likes.

"Hold on, get up," he says. He takes the red blanket off the back of the couch and spreads it over the white cushions.

"That was easy," she says. "You're so easy."

"We'll get more." He runs to get the condom, tearing at the wrapper with his teeth, while she removes her tank top and panties. She looks at her body and wishes the blinds kept out more light. Or it was dark out. And then he's kneeling in front of her and she's feeling for the ring at the base of his dick before guiding him in.

"Go slow," she says.

"I will," he says, plunging in too fast like he always does, but after that he's gentle. He looks at her like he might cry, says nothing more vulgar than how good it feels. Darcie holds his gaze for as long as she can and then buries her face in his chest, the hairs dry and graying; she breathes in his neck and shoulders and underarms, gets a whiff of his deodorant. She doesn't like to smell deodorant on him—it's like he could be any of the millions of men who use Speed Stick when she only wants his body above her, his weight. She puts her feet on his shoulders and grabs his ass, digs her nails into the backs of his thighs. She comes so easily for him, like she's never been able to do for anyone else.

At twelve o'clock, Darcie turns the sound back on and they watch the news. The Doppler radar shows pockets of rain all over central Texas.

"Bullshit," he says.

"I bet it evaporates before it hits the ground."

The weatherman says it'll be 107 again today and reminds them that the city enters stage 3 water restrictions on August 1st: no pools can be filled, no lawns watered, no cars washed except at commercial facilities or with a bucket of water filled directly from the tap. These things won't affect them but the rolling blackouts will. So far they've only heard rumors of

these blackouts. Darcie likes the sound of them. She went to
the dollar store and bought batteries and tall Mexican candles:
The Sacred Heart of Jesus, Our Lady of Guadalupe. Then the
weatherman talks about the fires in surrounding counties. He
gives them statistics she finds impossible to grasp—acres and
miles—numbers that seem preposterously large.

"Are you comfortable?" he asks, because she keeps moving
around, adjusting her pillow.

"Yes, baby. Are you?"

"Yes," he says.

She presses her body to his so closely that she can only
look at one of his eyes at a time. She stares at one of them
and then the other.

"I hope our baby has your eyes," she says. He can hardly
see anything without his glasses but his eyes are bright blue,
cracked and shining.

"I hope she has your wit," he says, which is maybe the nicest thing anyone has ever said to her, but then she wonders if
he finds her physical attributes lacking—what about her legs,
her ass? What about *her* eyes? And then she's annoyed but
feels bad about it.

"Hold on," he says, climbing over her again.

She watches him carry a chair over to the wall and stand
on it, press a button on the smoke detector. It blinks twice
and beeps. He makes some affirmative-sounding noises and
puts the chair back where he got it. And then he talks about
what they'll do when the end comes, which body of water
they'll claim for their own. It has become his favorite topic,
imagining the two of them together in a world that isn't like

this one. He tells her they'll take Hamilton Pool, which will provide shelter and plenty of fresh water, that this is their best option. They'll register the guns in her name.

At three o'clock, Darcie has to go to the doctor.

Since Terry's van is on empty and they don't want to spend the last of their money on gas, they decide to catch the bus. As soon as they step outside, they notice the haze and the smell of fire, which are new developments. Darcie is excited about these new developments until she thinks about what would actually happen if a fire came along and burned up all her stuff.

On their street, late-model SUVs are parked between cars with busted-out windows, black garbage bags filling the empty spaces. Some of the houses are in foreclosure and others are freshly painted with new roofs and yards full of flowers. The neighborhood is undergoing gentrification—about half the houses occupied by young white couples who are forever watering their tiny lawns and the other half full of people who would be described using words like *habitual* and *chronic*, with skeleton cars and underfed dogs.

Darcie doesn't know where they fit but she likes it here. It's like the whole world was thrown up into the air and everything got jumbled and nobody missed a beat, as her mother would say. There are roosters and chickens and dogs and babies and Volvos and former fraternity boys and gutted-out cars and old women in housedresses at three o'clock in the afternoon and it makes her feel like people might still be able to get along. The neighbors don't get along—it isn't uncommon to see them yelling at each other in somebody's front yard—but it makes her feel like it's possible.

They sit at the bus stop with a homeless guy who's not going anywhere and a man in a pink shirt. The man in the pink shirt stares in the direction that the bus is expected to arrive. Darcie stares with him. The homeless man's smoke blows past her face in a thick cloud. Sweat rolls down her back, her arms and legs, and she thinks about the clean white walls of their apartment, the space so small it gets nearly cold. She wishes she never had to go outside, never had to wear anything besides a tank top and panties.

Darcie takes Terry's hand and sets it on her leg, feels the heat and roughness through her thin dress.

The man in the pink shirt stands before she sees the bus rounding the corner; it pulls up right in front of her, right on time. It's her favorite driver, the friendly black man who waits when he sees her running and lets her off at red lights. The black women yell a lot and get mad if she asks questions and the old white men don't even turn to look at her when she gets on.

In the waiting room, Terry reads a magazine while she drinks water and fills out paperwork. Her bladder has to be full. She drank 32 ounces an hour before, just like the instructions said, but she peed. She wasn't supposed to pee, and now they're waiting for her bladder to fill back up again.

She takes her insurance card out of her purse, a private policy her parents pay too much money for every month. They used to pay her Chevron bill, too, but they stopped because there's a Chevron two blocks from their apartment and they

were going there three times a day to buy cigarettes and condoms and wine and toilet paper and plastic containers of fla-
vored noodles. It is an exceptional Chevron, filled with locally
made sandwich wraps and this fancy chocolate she likes, a
gold sticker sealing the box.

She leans over and looks at the magazine Terry's reading:
it's for men who want to discover the six things they don't
know about women. Terry is a good boyfriend in most ways
but he doesn't ask her questions about herself. He doesn't
seem curious about who she is and this bothers her when she
thinks about it, when she wonders if he remembers her sister's name, or what city her parents live in. When he asks her
something, it's about the immediate future: Does she want to
ride bikes? Go to the pool? Yellow Jacket? There's a barbeque
at Boone's house. Has she met Boone yet? She would like
him. He's good people.

Darcie turns in her paperwork and gets another refill.
Then she sits back down and drinks: the water sloshing in
her stomach. Terry puts his hand on her thigh and squeezes
down it in increments until he gets to her knee. She knocks
it off and elbows him as a pissed-off woman approaches the
desk. The pissed-off woman tells them she's late because the
place was hard to find and she's never been here before, and
asks why she has to pay to park in the garage. The woman is
well dressed, with careful hair and makeup. Darcie thinks she
must have been beautiful once, the kind of formerly beautiful
woman who had to find a different way of being in the world;
she probably imagines she's standing up for herself when
really she's just making everyone's day less pleasant.

"What if I always bleed during sex?" Darcie asks, leaning forward to sort through the fan of magazines on the table.

"It would be okay," he says. "We'll buy red sheets and red towels."

"No it wouldn't be okay. We'd have to fuck in the shower every time we wanted to do it." She locks eyes with the pissed-off woman's husband, who sets his magazine on his lap and looks at her.

"I bleed every day," Terry says.

"Are you being metaphorical? Please don't be metaphorical right now."

"No, I'm serious—I bleed every day. I fall off my skate-board or bike or cut myself shaving." They both know this isn't usually how he bleeds, that it's much less romantic—the ingrown hairs that fester and leak, the acne scabs she accidentally scratches open on his back. She looks at her breasts and adjusts her dress, her black lace bra peeking out. There is still plenty of time to fuck up and begin again before she has to figure out a different way of being in the world.

"What if something's actually wrong with me?"

"Then we'd deal with it." He waits a moment and says, "I'd never leave you."

It makes her want to prove him wrong. Of course he would leave; men aren't expected to stay. Her hair would fall out and she wouldn't be pretty anymore and he would leave, or he'd stay and hate her and she'd be forced to leave him. He pats her leg and says he thinks it's the condoms, which he's told her a dozen times already, and goes back to his magazine. She also thinks it might be the condoms. She's never really used them before, not consistently, and finds them strange and horrible.

Darcie watches two little girls run around while their mother rests her head against the wall. One of the girls is about six and so fat she has breasts. She has a violent look about her: a flop of hair covering one eye and a jerkiness like it's difficult for her to stop moving once she's started, or to start once she's stopped. One of the straps of her sundress slips off and Darcie waits for the girl's mother to open her eyes and set the strap back on her shoulder, brush the mop of hair out of her eyes. The younger girl is delicate and pretty, but neither of them is aware of it yet—how they are different, how their paths will diverge.

When Darcie's bladder is full, she tells the one in scrubs, and the woman leads her back to the sonogram room. She lifts Darcie's dress and tucks a sheet into her panties, squeezes warm gel onto her stomach.

"Have you ever been pregnant?" the woman asks.

"Yeah but it didn't take," Darcie says.

The woman waits for her to say more so she explains that she miscarried very early, that the doctor said most women wouldn't have even known they were pregnant. The woman asks a few more questions as she presses the wand to her bladder and then the clicking begins.

She alternates between closing her eyes and watching the monitor. She thinks of all the tests she's had over the years: a brain MRI, hearing and vision exams, screenings for depression, so much blood work. She has recently admitted something to herself—she actually *likes* going to the doctor. She likes answering questions about herself while someone takes notes. She likes waiting for the knock in a small clean room. She likes the free tampons and starter packs and she likes knowing all of the things she doesn't have, as if ruling things out can negate the things that are wrong with her.

"This must be a terrible job," Darcie says, "trying to do your work while a nervous person looks on."

"I love my job." The woman pauses to look at her. She's maybe twenty-five but hasn't kept her body up. Darcie wonders if she has kids at home, a husband. If she has a house in a neighborhood that has already been gentrified.

"Is all that clicking bad?" she asks.

"No," the woman says, laughing a little. "I'm just taking pictures. I'm going to have a look at your ovaries here in a minute."

After about five more minutes of clicking, it's clear the woman isn't going to tell her what the pictures show or don't show.

"Does anything look crazy?" Darcie asks.

"No, nothing looks crazy," the woman says, and that small laugh again. Then she tells her that the doctor has to go over the results with her, that he's the only one who can interpret them. Darcie watches the monitor for any large masses or asymmetry, but it could be perfectly normal or indicate certain death and she wouldn't know the difference. She asks herself if she's dying and listens for some inner voice to answer. It says no and she knows it's true, but now she's reminded that she will die, eventually, and she's upset about it. She doesn't want to die. She doesn't want to go about her days eating and sleeping and watching movies when she's going to die. It's ridiculous, this waiting for something else when this is all there is.

"Do you want to ride to Barton Springs?" Terry asks on the bus ride home.

Darcie puts her hand on his leg but it isn't enough so she grips his bicep with her other hand. She wonders how he can stand it, her constant need to touch him, to be near him. She wonders how long it'll take her to push him away but they've been together since Thanksgiving and he's still talking about their babies.

"Okay," she says. She listens to the inane conversation going on behind them, a couple of college boys trying to impress the blonde that's with them. One of them says, "I wish there was still a popular religion that had multiple deities," and the other asks if Hinduism counts and the discussion goes on all the way across the bridge, the blonde not saying anything. When Darcie was an undergrad, the boys were drunks who talked about pussy and action movies, and this new crop makes her miss these boys, who didn't pretend to be something else.

"Hey," Terry says, directing her attention to a fire truck on the side of the road, one of the men watering a charred area no bigger than a Pinto while the others look on.

At home, she changes into her swimsuit and then loads a backpack with towels and sunscreen, both cans of Four Loko, her driver's license and a magazine. She looks in the money drawer to see how much they have—twelve dollars in bills and quarters—and zips it up in the front pocket. Then she puts on her helmet and they carry their bikes down the stairs.

It's Friday afternoon and there's a lot of traffic so they ride on the sidewalk. Terry bikes ahead, looking back every so often to make sure she's okay. She's not good on a bike. All of the cars make her nervous.

They stop at a crosswalk and wait for the man to light up.

"This is the longest light in town," she says, adjusting her helmet. She looks at the grass, which is so dry it's turned a sickly yellow and crunches underfoot. When it finally rains the trees will fall, people say; there'll be dead trees strewn everywhere. Beads of sweat well up behind her knees and in the crux of her elbow, improbable places. Finally the man lights up and she gets her pedals into position and pushes off. What scares her about riding bikes is falling—she's terrified of falling. Other people seem to be okay with the possibility of injury.

When they reach the narrow path, Terry pulls his bike in front of hers abruptly and stops to let a man pass, her front tire bumping his back.

"Big tough guy," he says, when the guy's out of earshot.

"What are you talking about?" she asks.

"That guy's walk."

"Do you have a tough-guy walk?"

"If you have a walk like that they'll see you coming," he says. "You don't ever want them to see you coming."

They arrive at the free area where all the dogs are, where people drink beer and only wade out into the water to pee.

Darcie misses the three-dollar area, where there's water deep enough to swim laps. She can see it through the chain-link fence: still green water, people with their colorful noodles and floats.

She spreads their towels on a rock, carving out a little area among all of the other towels, and then sits and opens her magazine. Terry opens his Four Loko and leans back on his elbows, watching her. She can't concentrate with him watching but she doesn't look up—she wants to pretend she is self-sufficient, that she would be okay here alone. She reads an article about a man who found a lamp shade made of human skin after Katrina. He sold it at a yard sale and that person sold it to someone else until a journalist got ahold of it. The journalist discovered that a Nazi officer's wife had a fetish for things made of human skin—she particularly liked to make things out of skin that had been decorated with pretty tattoos. Darcie considers telling Terry about it but doesn't. He would say he already knows. In prison he read *The Diary of Anne Frank* four times. In prison he read constantly, everything he could get his hands on, and he hasn't opened a book since.

"I'm going down the water slide," he says, taking a long drink. The water slide is a little concrete ditch where the water pours in, but it's so low the kids have to use their hands to push themselves out. He doesn't move. She goes on reading her magazine. After a few minutes, one of his friends shows up, a girl named Amber. Wherever they go, he has friends. They're mostly girls—girls he went to high school with, girls his friends dated, girls who skateboard, girls who are friends with his sister. No matter how many Darcie meets there are always more, and nearly all of their names begin with the letter *A*—Allison and Alex and Andrea and Anna—and now this Amber, a pretty, ageing blonde unfurling her towel in the spot in front of them.

"This is my girlfriend, Darcie," Terry says. They shake hands and say it's nice to meet you and then Amber goes back to her towel and takes off her shoes with her feet. She steps out of her skirt and pulls her shirt over her head. She's too thin, with colorful tattoos blooming across her chest.

Terry asks about Amber's boyfriend and she says he's a great father but a terrible partner—they're splitting up—and then she's telling Darcie how he got her hooked on drugs.

Amber gives her the whole story—how they smoked crack on their first date and he said she smoked like a choo-choo train and then they were smoking every day and shooting heroin, too. Darcie looks at the dark lenses of Amber's sunglasses, glad she can't see her eyes.

Amber says she's been sober since the day she found out she was pregnant. Her boyfriend came home and she told him she was carrying his baby and they flushed the crack rock down the toilet together. She was never a crack whore, she tells them, gathering her fine hair into a ponytail. She was almost a crack whore but her boyfriend manned up. She gives Darcie the rundown of getting sober—sleeping for seventy-two hours, shitting herself—and says she still dreams of drugs. In the dreams, she can never get high.

"I dream I've got a needle as big as Terry," she says, "but I can't find a vein or all my veins are collapsed." She mimics trying to stick this Terry-sized needle into her neck, lifts one of her legs as if to scout out a vein there. "Or I dream a gigantic cartoon crack rock is chasing me." She pumps her arms and looks behind her to see if the rock is gaining. Darcie is reminded that she doesn't fit into Terry's world, that she doesn't fit anywhere except maybe at home with her parents, but she doesn't fit there either. Not anymore. She digs around in their backpack for the other Four Loko. She hates the taste but it has 12 percent alcohol and she can easily get a buzz off half a can.

Amber finishes her story, tightens her ponytail, and situates herself. Darcie watches as she lifts her hips into the air to adjust her towel, and then she watches Terry stand and wade out into the water. He cups his hands and pours the water over his head, rubs it into his face.

On their way home, they stop at Shady Grove. Terry doesn't want to spend the last of their money on beer when they could buy eggs and tortillas, but she insists. They sit at the bar and she orders a Blue Moon with a lemon while he drinks ice water. They look around at the other diners, mostly overweight tourists and old people at this hour.

Halfway through her beer, the lights go out. Everyone's quiet for a moment and then they're loud. Darcie's excited that they're finally going to witness a rolling blackout—it feels like the beginning of something, the thing she's been waiting for. She wonders if they have power at home and then she's thinking about the tall Mexican candles and the box of Popsicles in their freezer. She imagines standing on the street corner, handing them out to passersby.

She looks around at the other diners, the waitstaff—all of them looking around as if they are finally able to see each other, as if they are finally allowed to look.

"I like to call them *roving* blackouts," she says. "It sounds like an eye in the sky, like somebody watching."

"It's technically correct," Terry says, and then he starts talking to a man at the end of the bar and before long a man at a table tells them it's a squirrel, that a squirrel has chewed through a power line and this blackout may last awhile, until they can string a new line.

At home, Terry takes a joint out of his wallet and presses it into her hand. "Should we smoke it?" he asks.

"Where'd you get it?"

"Amber gave it to me."

"I'm tired of saving things," she says, wondering when she gave it to him, if he paid her for it, and if so, how. Darcie resumes her seat on the couch, looking out the window. Terry sits next to her and she leans over and bites down on his shoulder until she's sure her teeth marks will remain there for some time. He never tells her to stop or makes any sound at all, just waits patiently until she is finished doing whatever she's going to do.

He lights the joint and takes a drag, passes it to her. It burns better than the joints he rolls. She takes one more drag and he smokes the rest, leaves the roach in a glass candle-holder. And then he's talking about the time he fermented alcohol under his bed, paying twenty dollars for a pint of Blue Bell; he tells her about studying for his college degree and the guards who proctored his exams even though they weren't supposed to because he was on closed custody.

"I knew a lot of good people in prison," he says. "A lot of good people. I hope I never see them again."

And then the stories take a bad turn, as they always do, and he's telling her about the time a guard split a man's head open while they were on their knees, how that man was taken away and no one ever saw him again. He stands and paces, lights their last cigarette. She extends her arm, her fingers making a peace sign, opening and closing, and he passes it to her.

"You have to let it go," she says. "There's nothing you can do about it so you have to let it go."

"I know," he says. "You're right, I know."

"I'm serious. You have to."

"I know," he repeats. He walks over to the stove and opens the cupboard, takes out the flask. He unscrews the cap and drinks, offers it to her. She takes it and drinks and passes it back and he puts it away. But then he takes it out again and they pass it back and forth until it's gone.

Terry really believes the apocalypse is coming. She'd thought it was just a game they were playing, but it's not—he believes the end is coming because he wants it to come. When everything goes to hell, his skills will be useful again. He'll be high-ranking, not only carrying out decisions but making them. He'll adapt and flourish, which are things he's been unable to do in the straight world. They are also things she has been unable to do. Her friends from home are married, two children in. She can't talk to them anymore because they don't tell the truth: they tell her childbirth is beautiful and marriages only grow stronger; they ask her opinion on countertops and patio furniture and dishware, things that don't mean anything and yet they seem convinced of their importance.

They fall asleep on the couch watching a terrible low-budget show about skateboarders talking about skateboarding. When she wakes up, Terry's in bed. She would like to sleep beside him, but he twitches and says things loud enough to wake her and then she wakes him because he's woken her, because she doesn't like to be awake alone.

Darcie recalls bits of her dream—someone had broken into their apartment. She can see the man's eyes. She gets up and checks the locks on the door and then goes to the bathroom to brush her teeth. She tries to recall other things—where she was when she first saw him, how she would describe him for a character sketch. If she had to describe someone for a character sketch, she feels certain the man would never be found.

In this dream she woke up before he could get to her, but lately she's begun to die: the bad guy catches her; the gun goes off; she falls and doesn't wake before she hits the ground. She recalls a recent one in which she stood over her body outlined in chalk, a detective with his small pad taking notes. She went to her mother, who confirmed it. "You died," she said, "and we buried you, but you came back to life." Darcie told a few people about the dream just in case, so they could say she had predicted her own death, so they could say she had seen it coming. To know something's going to happen is almost like agreeing to it, she thinks, crawling into bed next to Terry.

ALWAYS HAPPY HOUR

"**A**re you going to take off your clothes when you go inside?" the boy asks. I have my usual swimsuit on, the white one. I have always wanted a white bikini and now I have one. The boy is in the shallow end in his Superman Speedo, the alligator Crocs his mother bought him that he refuses to take off.

"Little pervert," Richie says, squeezing the cherry from his cigarette, flicking his wrist. "Don't ask her questions like that."

I wrap a towel around my waist and go inside, walk the darkened hallway back to his mother's guest room and take my suit off. I put my dress back on—bra, no panties—and open the closet to look at his marijuana stalk: it needs another week to dry. *I could steal it,* I think, but he would give it to me. I don't really want it, anyway; it just seems like something that would be neat to have.

The boy wants tacos for dinner so Richie drives us to the store, the boy in the back strapped into his car seat. He seems enormous for a car seat, his long legs kicking.

It's cold around the meat and dairy cases. Richie pushes
the cart and the boy and I walk on opposite sides of it, watching as he fills it with fish, steak, tortillas, sour cream, and
onions; a box of Coronas, avocados, tomatoes, two different
kinds of cheese, chips and salsa—more than we need, enough
to waste. I cross my arms and suck the water out of a chunk of
hair. In the checkout line, I put a Diet Coke in the basket and
the boy hands me a candy bar and I put that in the basket and
then he hands me a pack of gum and I tell him to put it back
and Richie gets out his wallet. He always has a wad and he
peels off bills. He has no job, no income; he has no debit card
so he has to go to the bank during regular business hours to
withdraw money.

I take the boy's hand as we walk out to the car, and he lets
me hold it a second before pulling away. And then he jams his
hands into my sides while making a sound like *chicka chicka
chicka*. I laugh but it doesn't tickle. His father likes to stick his
fingers in my ribs. That doesn't tickle, either.

"Stop it," Richie says. "Don't play so rough with her." I look
at the boy, place my hand on top of his head, and he looks up
at me. I shrug. I don't know how to act around him. Richie
wanted us to like each other and now that we do, he wants
us to like each other less.

At the house, I put my swimsuit back on and go into his
mother's room to use the bathroom—she's in Tupelo this weekend, at a beauty pageant with Richie's sister and her two girls.
The toilet across the hall from the guest room doesn't flush
right and sometimes I have to fill the bucket with water and
pour it into the tank and I don't like to stay in the bathroom

that long. If I don't shit, if I'm pretty and don't ask too many questions, he'll love me. He'll tell me things—his thoughts and ideas, where his money comes from, what he does when I'm not around. Now he just tells me the worst things that have happened to him, same as he tells everyone, like the story of his father's race car going round and round the track and then crashing into a wall in a burst of flames as his entire family watched. He gets angry when people touch his arm, or look at him a certain way, and it makes everyone fall in love with him.

I peel the avocados with my fingers while he marinates fish, cuts the steak into strips. I dice onions and tomatoes and mash it together with a fork, add garlic salt and lime. Richie uses a separate bowl for everything: one for the sour cream, one for the chopped tomatoes, one for the shredded cheese, one for the salsa.

The boy dips an edge of a tortilla chip into the salsa, careful not to get any chunks.

"You don't like tomatoes?" I ask. He doesn't respond. "Tomatoes are the most amazing food ever." He's watching *Wolverine versus the Incredible Hulk* on the small television.

"Try the guacamole," Richie says. "Alice made it for you."

"Noooo," he says. He looks at me and then looks back at the TV: the Incredible Hulk smashes Wolverine with a boulder, and after the Hulk walks away, Wolverine—fully recuperated, not a scratch on him—surprises him from behind. Then they switch off.

"Which one is the good guy?" I ask, and I think about this guy I used to like, a former coworker I'd hung out with on

breaks, and how I thought he was going to be my boyfriend
but then he started dating a twenty-two-year-old—schooling
her in his various interests: scotch and acupuncture and Tai
Chi, things I might have actually liked to know something
about. I think of the time I straddled him at a party, how I
hadn't felt anything.

"Wolverine," the boy says.

"I thought the Incredible Hulk was a regular person, like a
researcher or something."

"They're both government experiments gone wrong,"
Richie says.

"*Wolverine versus Thor* is next," the boy tells me, and Richie
takes the fish outside to the grill. I watch him from the window, look at the sky: it looks like rain. I wonder what we'll do
then, how we will entertain each other.

That night, the three of us watch a show on the Discovery
Channel about a prehistoric creature that lived in the water.
From above, they show a ship and then a humongous black
thing swimming into the picture; it could tump it easily if it
bothered: everybody dead. They tell us how the creature lived,
how it might have died: diseases, sharks. Then they move on
to a bird that was shaped like a flamingo but much larger,
that could run fast and crush an animal's skull with one crack
of its beak, but it hunted alone and every time it laid its eggs,
wolves would eat them. The scientist-people recreate the
bird in steel and show its beak coming down on a honeydew
melon. They tell us that the honeydew melon has the same

consistency as the gray matter in our brains, which impresses the boy, but Richie and I get bored with the repetition, the same few scenes that stretch the show into an hour-long time slot. He reads *Time* magazine, a winding line of laid-off people on the cover, and I pick up one of his mother's watercolor books. It's an old lady book with step-by-step instructions and boring still-lifes. His mother probably paints fruit bowls and pastoral scenes—she is probably happy painting fruit bowls and pastoral scenes. I wonder what it would be like in her head—occasionally there'd be a thought like *I am nearly out of detergent* and then she'd write it on a list and it would go away. And then maybe an hour later, another thought would come along, something like *I wonder what comes on television tonight* and she'd get out the *TV Guide*. I wonder if she ever closes her eyes and sees the car going around the track, slamming into the wall.

When the show is over, Richie takes the boy to use the bathroom. Lately the boy has been peeing in the bed and they wake up with their legs wet. Every time he tells me about the boy peeing on him, I recall a drunken night in high school when a friend and I slept in my twin bed and I peed and blamed it on her. I told the same girl that the Ouija board said she was going to die in an accident nearly a year into the future and gave her the date. Only in retrospect is it possible to see I was a bully. I never thought of myself that way at all.

I pick up the remote control and flip stations, check out the reality TV shows I've been missing. At home, I don't have cable; I only have a small stack of DVDs I've seen so many times I have them memorized: *The Virgin Suicides*, *The Big Lebowski*, *American Beauty*, *Thank You for Smoking*. Sometimes I consider how The Dude would react, how he'd adhere to a strict drug regimen and go bowling.

They come back into the den and I look up at them and smile.

"Tell Alice good night," Richie says.

"Good night," the boy says. He puts his arms around me and I smell his soapy-clean hair and skin, then they go back to their bedroom where Richie reads to him from the book the boy gave him for Father's Day. On the cover, a father bear squeezes his cub, a pink heart above their heads.

I watch the dogs at the door, Richie's dumb friendly one and his mother's old deaf one that can't hear itself whine, and tiptoe into the kitchen to get a beer, open the drawer to look for a bottle opener. I'm trying to be quiet because I want the boy to go to sleep but I'm making a racket. Finally I find one and open the bottle, leave the top on the counter. Then I go back into the den and read about the laid-off people, everyday people who probably did their jobs as well as all of the other fuckups out there, but I can't concentrate because I start thinking about Richie and how I told him I loved him again—an accident—and how he held my face so I'd have to look him in the eyes and said, "And you know how I feel about you."

When I'm sure they're both asleep, I creep over to the doorway and find them facing away from me, Richie's arm around the boy. I touch my boyfriend and he opens his eyes.

He follows me into the den, puts his arms around my waist and rests his head on my shoulder.

"Walk me out?" I say.

"You can stay here," he says.

"I know, but I need to go home." I don't like sleeping in his mother's guest room, waking up alone in a bed decorated with seashells, paintings of boats and empty beach chairs on the walls.

We stand in the driveway and kiss. Then I get in my car and roll down the window.

"I'll call you tomorrow," he says.

I wonder if leaving will make him love me more. Maybe he'll feel like I'm slipping away, that I'll find someone else to watch television with and wander through the aisles of Winn-Dixie. I back out of the driveway, my windshield so foggy I can barely see. I try wiping it with my hand and then put the defrost on full blast and still nothing.

A policeman turns out of the gas station and follows me slowly across the bridge before turning off. He stays in his town, which is a nicer town separated from mine by a bridge.

Richie has an interview for a job teaching troubled kids, teenagers who have been taken out of regular school and put in a smaller, remedial school with the hope of transitioning back. He finished his degree in May and wants to use it, to stop working with his hands. Once, I overheard him tell my friend Gretchen that he was a carpenter by trade, which was something I didn't know, which was possibly a lie. He says the house he moved out of, the one in Florida where he lived with his family, was full of furniture and art he'd made and now it all belongs to his ex-wife. But his ex-wife lives here so I'm not sure what has happened to this house, if it's been sold, if it was ever theirs to begin with.

While I'm in class, he goes to the mall and buys a tie, dress shirts.

"I don't know how to tie a tie," he tells me over the phone.

"Ask your mother."

"I'll Google it," he says, and I wonder about his handshake. These are the two main things my brothers learned from our father: handshakes and ties.

I'm at home when he sends me a full-length picture he takes in the mirror: clean-shaven, collared shirt, tie, khaki pants: *Disguised as the enemy.* He calls immediately after to ask if I got it.

"You look like a regular boy."

"You mean man."

"Of course, a very manly man in a pair of Duck Heads," I say, which reminds me of an ex who wore khakis to work every day at his engineering job. We'd buy his Duck Heads at Kohl's and once a week, I'd iron a stack of them.

"Come over," he says.

I put my swimsuit in my purse, my toothbrush in case I spend the night. Then I drive across the bridge while listening to a Deer Tick CD he burned me. He burns me dozens of CDs he wants me to like, brings them over in envelopes with the songs neatly labeled. I stop at the gas station and pick up a six-pack, and then pull up to his mother's house, where he's mowing the lawn with his shirt off.

I pretend to read while watching him ride back and forth on the mower.

I think it's a night he doesn't have the boy but then his ex-wife pulls up in her shiny late-model SUV, and Richie drives the lawnmower over to the edge of the grass to greet them. I wonder where the money comes from, how there is always money when nobody works, and look at my old Honda parked on the street. His ex-wife: skinny with fake boobs and dyed red hair, a viney tattoo climbing up the back of her neck. She goes around to the passenger side and takes the boy out of his car seat, holding him on her hip like a baby. He has a camcorder in his hands. She puts him down and he shuffles over to where I'm sitting, drinking a beer.

"Does it work?" I ask.

"Of course," he says. He punches a button and the red light blinks on.

"Do something," I say, taking it from him. He climbs onto the lawnmower, hops off and kicks a tree. I point the camera at Richie's ex-wife, who says she'll be at the boy's soccer game tomorrow.

After she leaves, the boy goes inside to put his swimsuit on and Richie sits on the diving board, takes the pipe out of his cigarette box. The weed is dry now. He offers it to me and I shake my head. A couple of boyfriends ago, the other one I really liked, smoked pot every day. I smoked with him the first time and never did it again; it was something that made me different from the other girls he'd been with, the sad-childhood girls who'd had to be hospitalized after taking too many pills.

"You can come to the game if you want," he says. "Did I show you the shirts?"

The other coaches were happy being red or blue but Richie had his green shirts printed with a cumbersome, ridiculous name, something like Ninja Jujitsu Warrior Robots. "I don't want to be around her," I say. The way they constantly swap him has little to do with the boy or the boy's needs—I want to say this but can't. "Pass me that pipe." He covers up the hole on the side with his thumb as he lights it for me and then his thumb moves on and off while I inhale. I think about the circular box with metal teeth that my ex-boyfriend had, the nubs of joints in his ashtray, how he would collect a bunch and then smoke them, too. All of these things were called something.

I take another hit and the boy comes back out, walks over to the plastic storage bench and throws boards into the water: various sizes, with various superheroes on them. He doggy paddles to the deep end and grabs onto the diving board, shows me how he can pull up. His arms are so small and thin. I like the way they feel when he hugs me at night, before he goes to bed, before I fuck Richie quietly on his mother's couch.

"What do you want for supper?" he asks the boy.

"Tacos," the boy says, which is what he always says before he's reminded of his other options.

"What about hamburgers?" Richie asks.

"Yeah!" the boy says, pushing off.

"That okay with you?"

"I can feel all the muscles in my face," I say, touching my forehead, pulling at my cheeks.

"It's because you're smiling like that."

"I'm smiling?"

His mother comes out with one of her granddaughters, the younger pageant girl. She's blond and blue-eyed, wearing a lavender swimsuit with a ruffle around the waist. She walks over to me and points a tiny finger.

"Who is her?" she asks.

"Who is *she*?" Richie says. "Alice."

The girl turns and walks back to Richie's mother, who puts floaties on her arms. It makes me want a sassy beautiful little girl who will be a cheerleader and Homecoming Queen and Sigma Chi Sweetheart, all of the things I rejected outright because they weren't options.

"She's amazing. I want to steal her."

"I'll sell her to you," he says. And then, "I got something in the mail that says I'm supposed to get fingerprinted on Wednesday."

"That's good."

"I assume."

"They'll probably drug test you, too," I say.

He tells me he'll get something to flush his system, that he'll pass. I like this kind of confidence; even if he failed, I'd be impressed. He starts messing around with his plants, pulling off dead leaves, so I go to his bedroom and sit on his bed, take my swimsuit out of my oversized purse. I've slept in his bed once. The sheets smelled clean but felt dirty, just like I'd imagined. The next morning, he had to get up early to help a friend move but before he left, he kissed me and told me to sleep in and I felt loved.

I look at the guitars hanging on the walls, an expensive stringed instrument he brought back from India. He couldn't check it and had to hold it in his lap through the entire flight. There are bookshelves full of books, camping equipment, a piano, stacks of pictures and letters and clothes, his son's toys scattered across the floor. A life that once filled a house compressed into a room.

I swim breaststroke, counting to ten laps before letting myself rest. I know Richie thinks I should be playing with the kids or throwing the half-deflated ball to his dog instead of swimming back and forth. I try to keep the count straight in my head, but then I lose track and start estimating and then the boy pushes a board at my head and I stand in two feet of water. It feels strange for so much of my body to be exposed.

I hold the board steady while he kneels on it and then I let go and he attempts to stand while he's still wobbly and falls off.

"Get your balance first," I say. He tries again and again, doing the same thing each time, and then gives up. I look over at the girl.

"What's your name?" I ask.

"Keeton," Richie's mother says, and I watch her happily admiring her legs as they chop the water. If she were mine, we'd go everywhere together; we would never be lonely and she would renew my faith in humanity.

The boy hasn't done this for Richie.

"I hear you were in a pageant," I say, and she says something I can't make out and Richie says, "Tell her about your trophy, Keeton." She uses her hands to show me—round as a globe and tall as a skyscraper. I get out and lay a towel by the side of the pool, lie on my side and watch her drown the boy's dinosaurs while the water dries on my skin.

The next afternoon, Richie picks me up in his Bug and we drive out to the country. We pass convenience stores with handwritten signs advertising meat and cigarettes and God.

"I have anxiety," I say. My hair blowing everywhere doesn't help. I gather it to one side and hold it.

"Why?" he asks.

"I don't know why." *Because we drink all the time,* I think. *Because I've been having panic attacks for years but you wouldn't know anything about that because you don't know anything about me.* Lately I've been buying books about it: *The Worry Cure, The Chemistry of Calm.* The books say I have distorted thoughts, that these distorted thoughts create feelings, and these feelings result in my body's responses—shortness of breath, shaky hands, upset stomach, rapid heartbeat.

"Do you want my hat?"

"I'm fine." I twist my hair into a knot and tuck it into my shirt but it keeps blowing and I keep fooling with it and finally he takes off his hat and hands it to me. It's an old-man hat that has come back into style, a button on top and a mesh back. I saw Brad Pitt wearing one in a picture; he was on a child's bicycle, playing with his son in a lush green yard.

"Is my camera in the backseat?" he asks, as we pass another dilapidated barn. I try to breathe and look out the window at the wide flat yards and skinny pines, the houses set back from the road; three grubby children play on a stack of mattresses beside a mailbox. Other than the children, the country is eerily empty.

"Fuck it," he says, turning around in someone's driveway.

He drives up and down the main drag, my town laid out flat and ugly as a strip mall.

The patio at the Hog is mostly empty. We talk about a young lawyer-type in a suit, how pretentious it is to be wealthy and employed. Richie buys expensive shirts and then turns them inside out or cuts the labels off so he can pretend he doesn't care about money. When the waitress comes over, we order two-for-one screwdrivers and two dozen raw oysters.

"How'd the game go?" I ask. I light one of his cigarettes and look at the guy in the suit. He really *does* look like a dick. His sunglasses probably cost three hundred dollars.

"We lost."

"I thought y'all didn't keep score."

"There was a giant on the other team. There's no way that kid was five—I should have asked to see his birth certificate." The boy got discouraged and went and sat with his mother and when Richie tried to make him go back in, he cried and she took him to Pizza Hut.

Before, Richie says, the boy was handling it better than any of them, but now he wets the bed and cries about things four-year-olds shouldn't cry about. I don't know what's normal for a four-year-old to cry about.

"Do you think it has anything to do with me?"

"No," he says. "I think it has to do with him losing his home and his family and his friends."

To stop myself from touching him, I light another cigarette; hold onto my drink.

Richie calls the principal at the school for fucked-up kids but she's never available and she won't call him back. I don't know if he goes and gets fingerprinted. I don't think he does because he doesn't say anything about it and his fingertips look normal.

We meet for coffee before I have to teach composition to eighteen-year-olds, eighteen-year-olds who text during class and correct my grammar, who are nothing like I imagine I was at eighteen. Two weeks ago, Richie left a shiny red apple on my stoop to commemorate my first day, under an index card that said *Para Tu*. It's still on my desk, but eventually I'll have to throw the apple away and all I'll have is a card that says *For You*.

I usually get there before he does but I get stopped by a train so he calls and asks what I want and I tell him an iced coffee with soy and vanilla and then I get stuck behind a truck carrying chickens. I can see him from where I'm stopped at a light, at one of the little outside tables with his coffee, his book, and his cigarette. He's probably reading something I gave him, *Jesus' Son* or *The Dead Fish Museum*. I think about how I never call and ask what he wants but I should because he orders his coffee hot and has to wait a long time for it to cool.

I check my face in the mirror and then walk over to him and he explains that my coffee has vanilla soy milk and vanilla syrup and it may be too vanilla-y. He got me a large. I can't drink a large, but I like that he got me one. I open my eighteenth-century literature textbook to *The Country Wife* and close it again, my finger holding the place. I hate all the rhymed couplets, and I hate that whenever I point out the misogyny, the professor asks if it's a rhetorical device—was the author really a misogynist, or was he an egalitarian trying to call attention to misogyny?

"What do you have to do today?" I ask.

"Clean the pool, go to Home Depot," he says.

"What are you going to get at Home Depot?"

"I'm going to fix that toilet."

I think about the classes I'm taking and the ones I'm teaching, how far behind I'm getting even though school has just begun. I check the time on my phone and then go inside to use the bathroom. The pregnant girl is working. I dated her roommate, briefly, several months ago, but she wasn't pregnant then. I pretend I don't know her because I screwed her roommate over, because the whole thing is something I don't want to think about and now she works at the coffee shop closest to my house.

On Saturday, Richie picks me up, the boy in the backseat. I have a beach bag with three things in it: a magazine, a baseball cap, and a spray bottle of sunscreen. I didn't pack much because I know he will have packed whatever I might need. I'm wearing the wrong kind of shoes for the river and little black shorts over a black bikini. I'm nervous. As much as I like the boy, I can't get used to how things change when he's around: I shouldn't say shit or fuck or kiss my boyfriend; I'm supposed to pretend like he is the most important thing because he's a child.

"When are we gonna be there?" the boy asks. We aren't even on 49 yet.

"Soon," Richie says.

The boy bops me on the head with a foam sword and then slides it between my seat and the window, in and out.

"Leave Alice alone," Richie says. I don't want to be left alone. Don't leave me alone. I change CDs to exert some authority and look out the window at the old men on the side of the highway with their truck beds full of watermelons and tomatoes. I always think about stopping but I never have any cash. I hope these men will always be there, with their umbrellas, their overalls and homemade signs, and that one day I'll stop and buy a bag of sweet potatoes or tomatoes and say something about the weather, maybe, and the man will put his hands on his hips and look at the sky.

We pass the field of FEMA trailers leftover from Katrina: row upon row of uninhabitable boxes that the government is paying someone to store.

"Are we there *now*?" the boy asks.

"Two more minutes," Richie says, and the boy pokes me with the sword again and I grab it and turn around and smile, but my stomach is starting to hurt and all I can think about is whether I'll have to use the bathroom when we're on the river and how I'll manage it.

The boy and I wait outside the canoe rental place while Richie goes inside to pay. We organize his dinosaurs: which ones he should carry and which ones he should leave in the car, which ones to put in Richie's backpack. There are love-bugs everywhere. A couple land on his hand, and he holds it up and we watch them crawl up his arm. He's excited by how many there are and how they're attached, and I'm reminded that everything is new to him, and that some of this newness can rub off on me.

When the ones on his arm fly off, we watch a couple of sluggish single ones on the car window.

"Those two should get together," I say, and he agrees, and then Richie comes out with a waiver for me to sign that says no one will sue them if I die and then we gather our stuff and climb into the van. There's a family there already: a man and a woman, two boys and a yellow Lab, a whole complete unit of big people who seem perfectly content to take up so much space. Richie talks to them while I stare out the window. If I were alone or with another woman, it would be rude for me not to speak.

At the river, we let the family load up first while we coat each other in sunscreen and bug spray. Then we carry our stuff down to the canoe and get situated, the boy in the mid-dle holding onto the sides. We start paddling, looking for tur-tles and fish and redneck arrowheads, which is what they call trash. It's a game they started after the time Richie stepped on a piece of glass and sliced open his foot. At the first sand-bar, I walk up the hill to pee and return with a mud-encrusted 32-ounce beer can, drop it at the boy's feet.

"Redneck arrowhead!" he says.

"Redneck arrowhead," his father agrees. He picks it up and tosses it into the canoe and then the two of them walk into the river, to where the current is strongest, and Richie tells the boy to lie on his back and let his life jacket carry him downriver. I open my magazine, which has already gotten wet, the pages wavy and bloated. In the story, there's a lesbian couple in a Laundromat and they are having problems but they love each other very much and are going to have a party. The boy struggles, flips over onto his stomach. I keep reading the same paragraph again and again and then put it down and put my life jacket on, the cheap orange kind that looks ridiculous on someone with breasts.

I walk slowly out to where they are and sit in the water with my feet out. I take the boy's hand and we float together.

"It's fun, huh?" I say, looking at my tennis shoes. "Kinda freezing, though." When he starts to flail, I grab him and drag him back to the canoe.

Richie opens the cooler and takes out a beer, and I'm so relieved I could cry. I tell him I want one so he hands it to me and passes out sandwiches. They look fine, but they're soggy and have too much mustard and they make me think of all the good food I've eaten on canoe trips: potatoes and onions wrapped in tinfoil and burnt marshmallows, peanut butter and jelly sandwiches—the peanut butter and jelly mixed together until it is one even spread—stacked in a bread bag.

The boy brings me a rock and I set the sandwich on my knee. It is large and white, a rock-shaped hunk of concrete. I admire it before putting it in my bag so he goes and finds me more: black and white and bone-colored, shaped like teeth and eggs. Once I have a whole bunch, I pick up my bag and shake it so we can hear them rattle. Then we get back in the canoe and keep paddling. Soon we come to a rope swing surrounded by teenagers. Richie jumps into the water and puts his arms out, and the boy loops his hands around his neck and they swim over to the swing. I stay in the canoe, finishing my beer and watching them, and then I get out and walk the long way up the hill and around a downed tree to where an overweight boy is yelling at his girlfriend.

I stop to watch Richie and the boy fall into the water, the boy clutched onto him like a monkey. Usually I'm scared of rope swings, of heights in general, but it's easier when no one's paying attention.

The kid hands me the rope.

"What do I do?" I ask.

"You put your feet like this," he says, demonstrating, and then he moves one of my feet higher on the tree. He tells me to let go just as the rope starts to swing back, that that's where the water is the deepest, and I hold on tight and drop where he said to drop and it's thrilling—how brave I can be, how easily I can follow directions.

I adjust my top and swim over to Richie and the boy.

"Did you see me?" I ask.

"I missed it," Richie says.

"I did really excellent." I want to do it again, but Richie asks me to stay with the boy and swims back to the swing. The boy and I hold hands and watch as he does a flip into the water, a perfect easy flip, like something you'd see on television.

. . .

We're outside on the patio at 206 and it's happy hour again—always happy hour, always summer—my feet sweating in my Converse sneakers and my legs shaved all the way up. Tonight the boy is with his ex-wife and Richie's spending the night at my house so we can walk to the bars.

I'm drunk off two pints because I haven't eaten anything today but a piece of cheese and half an avocado.

"Happy hour's almost over," David says, and he lets us pre-order drinks, like he always does. Richie tips the difference, but that's not the point.

"I have to use the bathroom," I say, and I go inside, walk past the mostly empty tables and the bar, the ugly paintings and the elevator nobody uses. I stand in front of the mirror and look closely at my face and teeth to see if there's been any deterioration since the last time I checked. I put on more eyeliner. My sister says all a girl needs is eyeliner and a good personality, and I try to follow her advice even though I know she's completely deluded.

When I get back, Richie is talking to a guy named Peter, a guy who's here every afternoon in his paint-and-mud-spattered clothing. I say hi and then open Richie's silver ciga-rette case and take out his second-to-last cigarette. The night we met, I chain-smoked his cigarettes, though I rarely smoke, and he stopped at the gas station and bought me my own pack. The night we met, I was drunk and sucking on a piece of hard candy. I told him I was scared I was going to choke and he'd have to give me the Heimlich and he held out his hand and I spit the candy into it. Then he threw it behind his

shoulder and into a bush. And later he came up to my bedroom and got on his knees and lifted my dress and I made
him go home because already I loved him, because already
I knew it was the kind of love where you're so afraid they're
going to leave you give them no other choice.

LITTLE BEAR

Laura watches her kid slide down the slide again: three bumps and then dirt. It took her twenty minutes to talk him into it and now he wants to do it over and over. He has gone down the slide now thirteen times. She stands with her hands on her hips. She has lost all of the weight she gained when she had him and is proud of her body, which is mostly the same save for some stretch marks and a vagina that doesn't appreciate her husband's girth as much as it once did. After he comes, she finishes herself off with her pink rabbit. Sometimes, even though she's perfectly satisfied, she does it anyway and makes him kiss her neck and ears, anywhere but her mouth.

She checks her phone. It's after six o'clock and her husband should be home by now. She doesn't want to go home, but neither does she want to watch her child, Kevin, named after her husband, slide down the slide again. She imagines herself alone on an island. She would love it there. And yet she knows

she would grow tired of this lonesome island after a very short
period of time.

"Do it!" her son says as he scurries back up. "Do it to it!" It
is his new favorite phrase.

She wishes she had a friend with her but she seems to have
fewer and fewer friends, or her friends are busier or maybe
she's recently realized that they like their lives a lot more than
she likes hers so it's harder for her to be around them.

His joy at the bottom of the slide astounds her at number
sixteen, and she laughs as she picks him up. He feels heavier
than he felt only a few hours before.

"What have I been feeding you?" she asks.

"Hot dogs," he says, though she rarely gives him hot dogs.

She sees a bird with white wings fly into a tree and points
it out to him. The temperature is cooler—fall on its way, her
favorite season. But then Kevin kicks and screams to be put
down and she feels dulled and slightly disoriented, as if she
has no idea how she came to this place, this life.

"Again!" Kevin says. She wishes they had chosen some
other name for him. There is no good nickname for Kevin.
Mostly, she calls him Little Bear because the books he likes
best have bears in them. Last month, they took him out to
Yellowstone where they saw a black bear cross the road in
front of their car, just gallop across it like a dog. It wasn't
that big or menacing-looking, though her husband reported
it to be about 500 pounds. Yellowstone had been disappointing, overall. They were in their car the majority of the time,
making a slow loop—first the southern one and then the
northern—and traffic would frequently come to a complete

halt while people got out of their vehicles to photograph elk
or bison and Kevin had had to pee in bottles on two separate occasions, Laura holding his tiny uncircumcised penis.
On another, they barely got him to a toilet before he had an
accident. Old Faithful had not been particularly impressive,
though they'd had to wait for over an hour with a gang of
bikers and Japanese tourists jostling for position, and so, by
the time it went off, it wouldn't have been impressive even if
it had been.

Kevin took hundreds of pictures—never of the family
unless Laura specifically asked, but of the Grand Canyon of
Yellowstone and Yellowstone Lake and Hayden Valley and
the Grand Prismatic Spring—the best of which he posted to
Instagram (hashtag nofilter, hashtag familyvacation, hashtag
Yellowstone, hashtag summer). But she'd tried to be a good
sport because he'd done all of the planning himself.

Their hotel room had been very nice.

"One more," she tells him. "One more time and then I'll
make you a hot dog since you like them so much."

"No," he says. "Fifteen-sixteen thousand more."

"One more," she repeats, as he begins his ascent. She thinks
of the bear again, how it trotted on all fours. Her husband
hadn't been quick enough to get that shot.

She touches her stomach, as if she has just remembered
that she's pregnant, though it isn't possible to forget something like that. It's always there, like a slight headache or a
vaguely sore throat. She hasn't told anyone but her husband
and she only told him because she had to tell someone.
She expected him to be excited or disappointed, but he was

neutral. Well, he said, well, okay. That's good, right? And later that evening, he said perhaps the children would have to go to public school now.

What happened last time: bed rest, gestational diabetes, Netflix and Hulu and HBO GO and frozen pizzas and her husband, Kevin, who was at work most of the time, whose arrival she simultaneously anticipated and dreaded. But when he was more than half an hour late, she would text him repeatedly to ask where he was and when he'd be home followed by a series of question marks.

"Okay," Laura says, "that's it. That was the last one." She catches her son and picks him up.

"I don't like you," he says.

"Of course you like Mommy," she says. "You love Mommy." She smooths back his hair a little too roughly, her hand pulling through a knot. "Mommy is the best mommy in the world."

"No."

"You should get me a T-shirt," she says. "That way everyone will know how good I am."

"No," he says again.

She hopes this next child is a girl.

She buckles him into his car seat and starts the engine, but then she just sits there in the quiet, wondering how long it will take him to start screaming. She watches a black family set up for a birthday party. There are so many of them. There are balloons and hats and an older guy manning the grill and banners and children running about. A couple of the smallest children walk tentatively up to a girl with her dog. The girl smiles and they pet the dog and then they're all smiling and petting the dog. Laura wants to join them. She thinks of her own family, how they have spread out: both of her sisters in Texas—one east, the other west—her brother in Tennessee, their mother dead. Their father lives in Fairbanks, Alaska, where he moved to get away from them all, to not have to deal with them, though there was never much to deal with, she thought. Nothing so terrible. Her brother said he has a new family now, but she doesn't know anything about that. She wonders if he likes his new family or if he'll move someplace else soon and start over again with brand-new people, people who will seem so promising in the beginning. *There was nothing so terrible,* she thinks again, putting the car into reverse. There was nothing so terrible at all.

FIRST CLASS

We flew first class. We were drinking Perrier while the other passengers boarded. I looked at them and thought, *peasants*, as they bunched together with their overlarge carry-ons, bumping into each other and apologizing. Whenever Shelly and I went anywhere, it was always first class. We stayed in the best hotels. We ate in the best restaurants and she always paid. I had been hesitant about the arrangement at first. I'd offered to pick up tabs, pay my own way, but for Christmas she sent me a pale blue box from Tiffany's with a note that said *All my bitches have this necklace.* It was the nicest piece of jewelry I owned, a small diamond X.

Shelly won millions in the lottery; at the time, it had been one of the largest wins in history, though she'd had to split it with four of her coworkers (the press labeled them "the Super 8 Five"). Because she'd never had money before, she didn't know what to do with her wealth except spend it. She bought houses and cars and plane tickets and spent a lot of time ordering things online. She loved Costco and Target, which made her think of herself as unaffected. She didn't keep up with the other women but sometimes she Googled them to see if they were dead—one *was* dead, had died in a single-car accident a year to the date after the win.

It was the curse of the lottery, she'd told me on numerous occasions. Within seven years, 70 percent of winners were broke; there were stories of home invasions, murders, and suicides, and Shelly liked to follow them all. She thought she might write a book about it someday, a book that told *her* story, maybe even get in touch with the remaining members of the Super 8 Five.

This was the only thing I knew for sure about rich people: once the money was yours, it didn't matter that you hadn't earned it, had done nothing to deserve it; it didn't matter where it came from.

"We have to get you some new clothes," she said. "I'm tired of looking at that dress." When she tugged the hem, I noticed a wart on my knee. It had started out as a cut from shaving—I was sure of it—but I hadn't noticed the transition from cut-to-wart take place.

"I like this dress," I said, crossing my legs. "It's my favorite."

"I'm going to put you in a skirt. You never wear skirts. How come you never wear skirts?" And then she asked whether we should order mimosas or Bloody Marys. She liked for us to drink the same thing at the same time, though I always drank twice as fast and three times as much. She liked for me to do things when I was drinking, things she would never do.

When the flight attendant came by, I ordered a greyhound.

"Me too," she said, and I knew I'd displeased her.

Our relationship was affected in every way by her money; it was also affected by her looks, though she claimed she'd never felt beautiful because she'd grown up with acne and bad teeth, things that had long ago been remedied. Her adolescent sufferings made me want to connect with her, made me think we might eventually like each other in the way we claimed to in our emails and on postcards.

She offered me half a pill and I swallowed it without asking what it was: a benzo, I assumed. She put the other half back in her case, an opalescent gold-rimmed shell with a delicate clasp.

I touched the shell and said, "So pretty."

She tucked it back into her makeup bag and nestled her purse between us. She gave me so much and so freely that I was a little annoyed when she didn't give me everything I wanted. This was another problem with rich people: the more they gave you, the more you felt you were owed. It didn't make any sense—I knew she didn't owe me anything and yet I really felt like she should give it to me. And though she was generous to a fault, if I finished a bag of her Cheetos or smoked too many of her cigarettes, she was annoyed. One time I took her magazines down to the beach without asking and she didn't speak to me for the rest of the day.

She clutched my hand and closed her eyes. She hated takeoffs, which was most often when things went wrong, she told me, takeoffs and landings, as if this were knowledge particular to her. She pictured the plane exploding: boom, nothingness— you wouldn't even have time to come to Jesus. I took the opportunity to stare at her profile, her lips moving, cheeks flushed. Did she get filler in her lines? How did her skin stay so smooth and unlined even though she was a thirty-eight-year-old fair-skinned blonde? My other blond friends had begun to wrinkle in their mid-twenties, were sad when they got pregnant and had to forgo their Botox regimens.

Someone farted and I couldn't tell where it was coming from. And then the guy across the aisle opened a can of tomato juice and that smell blended with the other. He poured the juice into a cup of ice and swirled it around as if it were a fine wine before taking a sip. When he was done, he unwrapped a sandwich, something beefy and horrible, and I was disappointed because I thought things should be different in first class.

Shelly switched us over to Bloody Marys. She asked for extra olives and celery, extra everything, which I also wanted but didn't ask for. I was jealous—she had a side cup full of veggies, fat green olives with their little spears—but I couldn't bring myself to ask for one of my own even though the flight attendant was right there and ready to serve me. I tried to recall how long I'd been off my daily anxiety medication and whether it was possible that this had something to do with it. I didn't think this kind of thing would have bothered me before. By all accounts my transition off meds had gone smoothly but I'd begun to notice small things: I didn't strike up conversations with strangers as easily or smile at them; I didn't ask for things as readily at restaurants and many of the tables felt too exposed. I was beginning to be afraid again.

. . .

The hotel was bright and modern.

There were two bedrooms, each with their own private bathrooms, and a sitting area with a fireplace. There was a balcony looking out at the water. Everything was spotless but Shelly had brought along a package of disinfectant wipes, saying she'd seen an episode of *20/20* in which they'd done tests and found that shitty hotel rooms were no more dirty than the expensive ones—fecal matter everywhere. Everything she said was obvious and boring. Of course nice hotel rooms were just as dirty; rich people weren't any cleaner than poor ones. They might be neater, more conscious of hiding their evidence, but they weren't cleaner. I recalled the last hotel I'd stayed in, a four-star with my parents on the coast, and how I'd just settled into the bath when I noticed streaks of blood above the waterline. I'd stared at them for a long time, considering whether they had been smeared there on purpose—they certainly looked purposeful, three fingers' worth—and how the cleaning lady had missed it. But I hadn't called housekeeping or wiped it off or anything. The following day I took a shower.

I counted the nights I had to be with her: four. It seemed like forever and I wondered how I'd found myself in this situation when I promised myself every time it would be the last, swearing that I wouldn't put myself in her debt again, but here I was. She had her ways. She spaced the trips far enough apart for me to forget how miserable they were and so far in advance that I could imagine they wouldn't ever happen, or we'd be different. But each time we were the same people who fell into the same roles and by the time the trip was over we hated each other. I had no idea why she kept planning them. It seemed a sort of sickness.

I sat on the couch and changed channels while she cleaned, the smell of lemony chemicals. Then I went to my bathroom and washed my face, took the toiletries out of my bag and placed them around the sink. There were fancy soaps and shampoos and mouthwash, Q-tips and cotton balls in silver containers. I cleaned my ears but they were already clean. I squirted some lotion into my hands and rubbed.

"I need a fan," she said, when I resumed my place on the couch. "I can't sleep without white noise."

"You usually bring that little machine."

"Derek uses it."

"No prob, Bob." I called housekeeping. After a guy brought the fan and she took it to her room, she had me call again for toothpaste and then extra pillows—she needed at least four pillows if she was alone. She gave me tip money and I answered the door to the same guy each time: well over six feet tall and slightly too thin, handsome. If he was annoyed, he didn't let on. He called me Ms. Nugent, my friend's name, and I didn't correct him. Between his first and second visits, I put on lipstick. Between his second and third, Shelly suggested I blow him; she would give me five hundred dollars to blow him. I changed into a short strapless dress and imagined blowing him.

"Thank you," I said, as he put the pillow in my arms. It was oddly intimate. Five hundred dollars, I thought. What I might do with five hundred dollars.

In a different context, he might have been my boyfriend. I had a boyfriend but I couldn't stop myself from wanting others. It was a pattern. I'd start thinking about something small, like how my boyfriend didn't cut his toenails but enjoyed pulling them off with his fingers, among other shortcomings and failures, terrible things he'd once said or done in anger or passion, and then I'd wonder how I could ever be with this person, just the two of us alone together in a house for years. What would we say after a while? I couldn't imagine any scenario in which we might be happy. I guessed the one thing I couldn't understand about life was why no one seemed to be with the person they loved most in the world.

Shelly opened the fridge and took out two mini-bottles of white wine. She handed me one and we clinked them together.

"I bet he had a really big dick," she said. Then she said she needed a bath and went to her room and closed the door. We both loved baths and never showered. It was one of the things we had in common.

I took her pack of Davidoff Superslims and went out to the balcony. She always had cigarettes, though in all the years I'd known her, I'd only seen her smoke a few times.

There was a sign in the room that said smoking wasn't allowed anywhere on hotel grounds—there was a $250 fine—but if I was caught Shelly wouldn't mind paying. She would probably be happy to pay a fine and would enjoy telling people that we had gotten into trouble. Like many people who'd grown up without much that suddenly found themselves with more than they could spend, she seemed desperate to return to her original state. Every six months she put on a dress and met with a man who gave her figures and charts and tried to talk to her like a father. She was spending too much, he said, the money wouldn't last forever at this rate. She told me she'd been happy before the money and would be happy without it, but I couldn't believe this at all. What would she do? Go back to cleaning motel rooms? I wondered how much was left and how long it would last and whether Derek would stay with her if she was broke. I imagined her back at the same Super 8: highlights grown out, looking her age and older, old. I didn't want to see that. I had genuinely liked her at some point, many years ago.

I lit another cigarette and watched the smoke blow to my left. I could hear people to my right and tried to make out what they were saying but they were speaking in voices too low to hear.

They were angry; people liked being angry. They liked fighting and making up and feeling like a button had been reset, like they could start fresh, or perhaps it was just one more nail in the relationship coffin and another step closer to done. I wondered what people were doing in this hotel, which is what I always wondered in hotels, or when traveling, in general. Why had they come here? Were they happy? It made me think of my honeymoon and how I'd cried and told my husband that the marriage had been a mistake and then he'd cried and said maybe it had been and it made us feel better. We'd stayed together seven years.

Soon Shelly would be finished with her bath and we would

go to the CVS where she'd buy kitschy ashtrays along with her junk food. She'd buy t-shirts and postcards that said MIAMI in different-colored letters. These trips, more than anything, were about proving that she traveled and had friends. She'd sent me postcards and T-shirts from all over the world. I wore one of the shirts often: ARUBA, it said, thin and slick between my fingers because I'd washed it so many times. On the occasions I'd worn it out of the house, people asked me what Aruba was like and I said it was a beautiful place with very pretty women, that we'd rented a Jeep and driven from one side of the island to the other, climbed to the top of the lighthouse. I told them that my boyfriend left the hot young cleaning lady large tips every morning even though he was cheap and had never tipped a cleaning lady before.

I texted my boyfriend, told him I'd arrived safely. I asked if he wanted to see a picture of my bruise. A little over a week ago, I'd fallen down the stairs and bruised my left thigh; it had spread and the colors were glorious.

I don't need to see the latest, he wrote back. You know what I like. I *did* know what he liked; he was very forthcoming about what he liked. Around the house he liked for me to wear shirts that barely covered my ass. He also liked it when I baked cookies. I sent him a picture of the bruise anyway, which looked ugly and more horrible than it did in person. He didn't respond. Then I went back inside where Shelly was standing in front of the TV in her bikini bottoms.

"I need you to help me apply this tanner," she said. "I meant to get a spray-on but ran out of time."

All she had was time. She didn't work. I had time, too. I

was in my third and final year of graduate school, was older than all but one of my classmates.

I had seen her breasts on a number of occasions but I always liked to see them again. They were round and nice but her nipples were too dark. I liked pale nipples, nipples one shade darker than one's skin color, like my own. She handed me the mitt and the foam and told me to rub it in good.

"Do you want me to do you?" she asked, when I'd finished.

"I don't think so."

"We need to be tan," she said.

When I was around her, I felt heavy, short. I wasn't heavy or short but she was tall and wore heels that made her taller and never gained weight despite her diet, which seemed to consist solely of candy bars and chips. I thought of it as an endearing trait, her love of processed foods. And though she ate these things, she counted every calorie, had figured out how to do it without gaining a pound.

"Okay," I said, "you can do me." I pulled my dress down and hung it on the back of a chair. I raised my arms and stood with my legs apart.

"Jesus," she said. "What the fuck is that?"

"I told you I fell."

"I didn't know it was this bad. Jesus," she repeated.

"I know. It's awful, isn't it?"

"Does it hurt?"

"Only when I touch it. I hope it heals okay."

"Well," she said, and I could see that this bruise, which really was huge and horrible, had depressed her. We weren't going to look as good in our bikinis as she'd hoped. And I was sure I was fatter than the last time she'd seen me. Every time, I convinced myself I was fatter than the last time she'd seen me.

She rubbed the tanner in thoroughly, gently, not just on and around the bruise, but over my entire body. "Maybe this'll hide it some," she said. "It'll be fine." I hated self-tanner, the way it smelled, the way my ankles or knees always looked wrong. I thought of a crime show I'd watched in which a man claimed his wife had an allergic reaction to a self-tanner and it had killed her. It was so preposterous that many people believed it, at least until they'd gotten all of the test results back.

We waddled around with our arms flapping, legs spread, and then I slipped my dress back on and she began to take pictures of herself. She was always taking pictures of herself and posting them to her Instagram. Most of them appeared to have been taken by someone else and I often wondered who was behind the camera, if she had a tripod she set up. She looked sexy in these photos, hair falling in her eyes, lots of skin. I hardly ever posted new photos or took them or even agreed to be in them because all of the personas I put on felt wrong. I didn't feel sporty or nerdy or sexy. I wasn't pretty or ugly enough, fat or thin enough. Eventually I wouldn't need to construct any persona at all. I would just be old.

She went to her room to get ready. I tried to read one of the books she'd mailed me months ago. She was always passing along her favorite books, telling me what movies to watch and music to download, but recently I didn't want to read or listen to or watch things I hadn't read or listened to or watched before.

The book had an unattractive cover of a lady in a big coat holding a bird. I turned it over and read the blurbs again. I read the author bio for the third or fourth time and stared at her picture. It was a picture she'd used for decades.

"Are you ready?" she asked. She looked amazing and effortless, but I knew she had carefully planned this outfit, perfectly casual yet nice enough to wear to a fancy restaurant. It was all a performance and it was all for me. I was wearing an unfamiliar bra that dug into my side fat and the slutty dress. I'd forgotten to pack my knockoff Spanx so I had to stand up as straight as possible and suck in my stomach but my makeup looked pretty good. My boyfriend said he liked natural women, but it wasn't really what he liked—it was only what he wanted to like. Perhaps it made him seem like a nicer guy to himself.

We went down to the hotel bar and took the last two stools, opened the enormous drink menu between us. We had to hold it right next to the candle to read it.

"Let's order something tropical," she said. "Pineapple or mango."

"I'll have whatever you're having." I wondered how many times I'd said this in my life, but people were always ordering things I wanted. It was better this way.

Our drinks came. We toasted Miami and told each other "We're in Miami." This was also part of it—we would remind each other where we were and how beautiful and exciting it was, how nice it was to be away from home, even though nothing ever seemed exciting or beautiful when we were together. I wished we were in Las Vegas. In Las Vegas, no one expected you to gamble with them; you could slip away to the bathroom and be lost for hours.

I dipped my fingers into the wax while she watched, horrified. I blew on them and then lifted each one off, carefully, lined a little wax family up on the bar. It reminded me of the sticker people and pets you saw on the backs of vans and SUVs.

"I want to go to DASH and see Kourtney," she said. "She's my favorite."

"You have a favorite?"

"You don't?"

"No."

"Come on," she said.

"I guess Khloe seems like the most fun?" I very much doubted that we would be seeing any of the Kardashians. If they ever were in the store, it was probably closed.

"We have to buy something there—maybe we'll find you a skirt."

"I'm not crazy about skirts. You have to have something to go with it. You have to have like an outfit."

I always bought stuff on these trips because Shelly didn't like to be the only one buying things. On our last trip, I'd paid eighty dollars for an oversized tank top with a studded star on the front.

"The men are all looking at you," I said, craning my neck around. Perhaps if she thought she was the most beautiful woman in the bar she'd be in a better mood.

"They're looking at *us*. They probably think we're lesbians." She pretended to whisper something in my ear and then tossed her hair and laughed.

She had dated women, had been in love with women, but said she was never sexually attracted to the ones she knew well or considered friends. And she would never end up in a long-term relationship with a woman. Women were for fun—they weren't actual prospects—who would take out the trash and do the taxes and whatever?

"This drink is really strong," she said. "I think I'll get a glass of wine." I'd finished mine so I started drinking hers. She gave me a squinty-eyed look and said, "I still might drink it."

She didn't want me to have the things she wasn't going to use; she would rather throw them away. My sister had a rich friend who took all her old clothes to Goodwill, often with the tags still attached, rather than give them to her friends. What if she saw my sister wearing a shirt she'd bought and decided she wanted it back? She would realize it was cute and she ought to wear it, that she had made a mistake. My sister also went on trips with her rich friend, but she paid her own way.

We were hungry so we ventured out to find something to eat. We weren't the kind of travelers who researched things beforehand, and neither were we the kind to engage strangers in conversation about where we might go. We walked past hotels that looked a lot more fun than ours, young people laughing on patios, music playing. Shelly always picked the nicest but beigest places, where all the old white people stayed. She liked to be the most attractive person wherever she went and coordinated her life to make this happen as frequently as possible. She didn't seem to understand that she would be the most attractive person wherever she went. She didn't need to surround herself with geriatrics.

After some back and forth that grew increasingly unpleasant, she walked into a restaurant and I followed. We were already annoyed with each other and the vacation had just begun. When it was over I would be exhausted and fragile. My tan had turned out well, though, the best fake tan I'd ever had.

While we ate, we settled on a neutral topic that seemed to put us both at ease—her son—it was always hard for me to believe she had a child and had raised him nearly into adulthood. He would be going away to college next year and she was already devastated. He had a girlfriend named Sarah that he was sleeping with. He played baseball. I'd seen a movie where the men come and go so frequently in a mother's life that a boy throws the ball to one man and it's returned by another, but I couldn't remember the name of it. Over and over, the men changed: a clean-cut guy in a suit turned into a plumber and then a hippie and then a college professor. I imagined this was what her son's life had been like, at least when he was younger. She'd been dating Derek for a number of years now but wouldn't marry him; he had asked on several occasions and she'd said no, offering him feminist reasons that neither of them believed. To me she said she didn't think she was "in love" with him anymore, that she wasn't sure she ever had been. She said when her son was gone, perhaps she'd get rid of all of it: the man, the house, the city, and start over. We had this in common, too. I just had less to disassemble.

. . .

When I got in bed I was a little drunk. I piled the pillows around me and thought about how comfortable it was, how soft the sheets. Then I called my boyfriend to tell him I was having a terrible time.

"That's why I never go anywhere," he said. "People say they like to travel but then they get somewhere and just want to go home."

"Not everyone," I said.

"Well," he said, "you do, every time."

"It's hard to fully appreciate home unless you leave it."

"Not me," he said. "I know what I have here." I imagined him looking around his living room. He was on the couch with a bowl of popcorn, an action movie paused mid-fight scene. Maybe he'd have an ice cream cone before settling into his king-size Tempur-Pedic. He was by far the dullest man I'd ever been with. "I'm happy here," he said, "I don't have to go anywhere else to be happy."

I told him that was nice and said good night, goodbye. We didn't say I love you and I wondered if we ever would; every day we didn't say it seemed like one more reason we should never say it. We'd been dating close to a year. I liked him most when we kissed, but only the closed-mouth kind when we pressed our lips together hard.

I turned on the TV and searched for something that might be interesting enough to hold my attention, but not so interesting that it would keep me awake. Something I had seen before. I fell asleep watching *Back to the Future Part II* and woke up with it still on, remembering my dream. There was a man and his wife and another lady, all of them middle-aged and dowdy. They were in the lady's house, getting ready for church. The man and his wife said cruel things to each other while the lady put on her makeup and then filled a to-go cup with coffee. The lady said that maybe she and the wife could spend the day together after church? Leave the man on his own? And the man agreed. He said his wife had never had a friend in her whole life. And that was it, the entire thing. It was so on-point that it wasn't like a dream at all.

I woke up at eight o'clock and went back to sleep. The later I slept, the shorter the day would be. I awoke again at nine-thirty and read a few paragraphs in the book with the bird lady before running a bath.

I was dressed and ready to go at eleven when Shelly finally emerged from her room and suggested we walk to Starbucks. Like Target and Costco, Shelly also loved Starbucks. She got angry when people talked badly about any of these companies' market shares or poor business practices because how far did it go? Should we *only* buy from places that sold products that were made fairly and responsibly? That paid their workers decent wages and were environmentally friendly? Because, if so, there'd be nowhere to shop and then what? She was a smart person but she had difficulty with degrees.

We walked around with our coffees, peering into store windows. I was slightly hungover and one coffee wouldn't be nearly enough. She wouldn't drink all of hers but I couldn't have it.

"What do you feel like doing?" she asked.

"I don't know. I'm not sure yet." I didn't know anything about Miami. I'd just gotten on a plane with a suitcase full of bikinis and flimsy dresses and less than thirty dollars in cash.

"Maybe we could go to the zoo," she said. "I bet there's a good one here."

"I don't want to do that."

"Why not?"

She liked zoos and I didn't and we had a short but ugly conversation in which I told her about a couple of pandas I'd seen at the zoo in Atlanta, slumped over barrels and panting in the summer heat, how I'd wanted to shoot them in the head to put them out of their misery.

We stopped at CVS and she bought mini-Snickers and Doritos and Sprite Zero, two bags of gummy worms, three ashtrays and ten postcards and two T-shirts and three magazines and a four-pack of lip gloss in the cool family. She considered a bunch of other things and I stood there and looked at them with her. This was how she spent her days, going from one place to another to buy mass-produced items she didn't need.

When we got back to the hotel, she went to her room and shut the door. I heard her on the phone with her boyfriend so I opened a bottle of white wine—it was so cute—and sat on the couch, waiting for her to come back out. I waited a long time, nursing the bottle.

"Want to go to the pool?" she said, emerging in a stars-and-stripes string bikini. It reminded me of the Coca-Cola one-piece I'd worn as a child.

"Sure. Everything okay?"

"He's being a dick." Usually I loved hearing the awful details of people's relationships because they made me feel better about my own, but I felt sorry for Derek. "He hates it when I leave."

"I know," I said. "They can't do anything by themselves." My boyfriend was fine by himself. There he was on his couch, everything within reach.

Since she was originally from South Dakota, she didn't mind that it was windy and 68 degrees, that we were the only ones in our swimsuits. The sun was shining and that was enough. There was a guy selling hamburgers and drinks at the poolside bar.

"Hello, ladies," he said. "Can I get you anything?"

"No, thank you," I said, averting my gaze. I really had to go back on my meds. I vowed to do it as soon as I got home.

He said to let him know, that he was there for the duration. Shelly caught my eye and winked.

"Cute," she said. "You should fuck him."

I smiled as though it was a possibility. We situated our magazines and bottles of white wine and I thought about how I would associate them with this trip long after it was over because I never drank white wine at home, and certainly not in these little bottles. She hadn't opened hers yet. I would just watch it perspire. On the last trip we'd taken, we'd ordered cheeseburgers and fries from room service one night and she'd removed her bun and eaten exactly half of the fries. And that was the real difference between us; she had a very complicated system she adhered to without fail no matter how she felt. She did, however, confess to crying a lot and I never cried. I couldn't remember the last time I cried. I didn't understand criers or how I could be one of them and if the crying might substitute for some of the bad feelings and the bad things I felt compelled to do because of them.

The wind picked up and then the clouds covered the sun. I put my shirt back on. I looked over at her, still and thin in her American bikini, one arm above her head so her ribs were more prominent. In New York—our last trip—two of her other bitches were with us so it had been easier; I wished they were here now. There had also been museums and streets crowded with people, places to get lost. The clouds gathered and gathered and then it started to rain and there was nothing either of us could do about that.

Back in our room, I went out to the balcony and smoked her cigarettes and wondered why I didn't have my own. Why I hadn't pulled out more cash before getting on the plane. Why I got myself into situations I didn't want to be in and then stayed in them for so much longer than was necessary. Did I just like to torture myself? And, if so, what could I do to change this? I checked my account balance on my phone and called the airline, but I'd done this numerous times before and already knew that the cost of the changed ticket would be comparable to the price of the original, which would be more than I could spend. I hung up before I connected with a human. I would have to wait this one out and remember this feeling when she asked me to go somewhere the next time, as she would, even though it seemed impossible, ridiculous. She didn't like me and it was hard to like someone who didn't like you. Or I didn't like her. Or we were too similar or too dissimilar or it was just a bad match. It didn't matter. I fingered the small diamond X around my neck, which I never wore at home, and tugged on the chain. Then I tugged a little bit harder. It didn't break and I was glad of it. In movies people chucked their wedding rings into the ocean and their cell phones out of car windows, but I'd never heard of anyone doing this in real life; in real life you held onto things as hard as you could because you knew how difficult they were to replace.

CHARTS

"I'm going to marry him," my sister says, standing in my kitchen. I don't want her in my kitchen. I wonder if she can feel me not wanting her in my kitchen.

"Do you love him?" I ask.

"He's wonderful. He loves me so much."

"That's not a reason to marry him."

"No," she says. "It's not." She takes the Lean Cuisine out of its box and tosses the frozen entrée onto the counter. "But that's not the reason."

I unwrap my burger, scrape a corner of cheese off the waxy paper. I've found a whole system that allows me to eat the things I want and not get fat. I worry. I weigh myself every morning, before coffee, after I go to the bathroom. Sometimes I throw up. I'm underweight by some charts.

She stabs a fork into the plastic for ventilation, presses buttons on the microwave. I want to say, *Forget that, let's go out.* I want to link my arm through hers and go traipsing down a dark alley, half-drunk on tequila, but I'm not this person. I

thought I could be once, by moving to another city or medi-
tating or doing any number of other things. *Try pretending*, the
books said, *act for long enough and eventually you won't have to
act. It'll just be who you are.* I once met a girl who wrote these
books, a ghostwriter. Her case studies were her family members; she did her research on the internet.

I use a napkin to remove the excess mayonnaise, leaving a
fine layer on the bottom half of the bun. I remove the onions
and pickles and a thick, pale tomato—a winter tomato an
ex-boyfriend used to call any tomato that wasn't bright red
and bleeding, the only thing left on his plate.

My phone rings; it's our mother. I hit decline even though
it's the second time she's called today and she panics when I
don't answer twice in a row—she thinks I might be dead—
but I talked to her yesterday and felt bad about myself for an
hour, at least. The thing I hate most is how I can never recall
what she's said that upset me so much. I try explaining it to
people and I'm the one who sounds like an asshole.

The microwave dings.

"Have you talked to Mom today?"

"Yesterday," she says, "I called her from the airport. I usually call her when I've almost gotten to the place I'm going so
I can't talk long." She hops onto the counter with her tray and
looks out the window. It's how I eat when I'm alone. There's
a lot of counter space and the backyard is full of pecan trees
and squirrels, neighbors moving behind the slats of my fence.
I like to watch the squirrels bury their nuts. I like it when
they catch me watching and give me a long hard look like

they will fuck me up if they have to. I paid for this house with my divorce money: two bedrooms, two bathrooms, and an office. A backyard. A big open kitchen connected to the den and plenty of light. I still can't believe it's mine. I feel like I'm house-sitting, like the owner will be back any minute and will be disappointed because the plants are half-dead and there are dirty socks everywhere.

"What should we do later?" I ask.

"I have to meet some people for a drink," she says. "It won't take long. You're welcome to come."

My sister has more friends in this town than I do. I don't know how it's possible, seeing as she's never lived here. I only know one of them, her freshman-year roommate, Leah. We've run into each other a few times. She's tan year-round and wears loose clothes and jangly bracelets.

"That's okay, I'm pretty tired."

"What are you going to do?" she asks.

"Watch *Mad Men*, probably."

"I haven't seen it."

"It's really good, you should watch it."

"I'm too busy to get into a series right now," she says, and sighs like her busyness is something she doesn't want, though she has always loved creating errands for herself, making plans with too many people in a day so she never has to be alone.

She twists her hair on top of her head and it stays there, a great big knot.

My sister and I are both adopted. She looks like our parents—blond and tall and large-boned. No one would ever know she was adopted; people can't believe it when they find out. They say, *But she has his nose, her mouth.* She even walks like them.

My skin is olive; my eyes are shaped like almonds. At thirty-three, I finally like my olive skin—it hasn't wrinkled like my sister's. My forehead is smooth and unlined. I only have the tiniest beginnings of one crease on the left side of my mouth. I must smile crooked or something. There are other things: I never had acne; my standardized test scores were always higher. No matter how much smarter I am, though, how much better, I'm the one who doesn't fit.

"I could eat like four of these," she says, hopping off the counter and stepping on the trash can's pedal. She drops the tray in and opens the refrigerator. "Do you eat every meal out?"

"Not every meal."

She opens the freezer, closes it, and looks at me. I can't stop noticing her left hand, which is calling attention to itself in a way it never has before. Her diamond is large, princess cut. As a teenager, she bought wedding magazines at the grocery store, kept them under her bed in great dusty stacks. Some-times I looked at them with her and we'd pick out dresses and cakes, but I never pictured a man attached to any of it. And then I got married at twenty-two while she went on to get advanced degrees and travel the world, making friends all over. She even taught in South Korea for a year.

The man my sister is going to marry isn't good enough for her. He seems like a guy you might pick up at Target, the kind who took a break from shopping to sit in a plastic booth and eat popcorn. It's not that she's gorgeous or anything, but she's magnetic. If she were on a TV show and America had to vote, she'd win. *She's got star quality,* they'd say. *She's got that "it" factor.*

"You should come with us," she says. "These girls are really nice—they could be your friends."

"I know Leah."

"Yeah, Leah likes you. Y'all could be friends."

"I have friends." I wonder why she's here, why she's come. If I asked her, though, she'd act confused. She'd say she missed me. She'd say she wanted to see my house, which is so lovely.

My sister lives in an apartment. She complains about the girls who live above her—they wear their high heels inside, their dogs cry every time they're left alone. I've never been to her apartment, never seen these girls, but I can picture them. They're blond, like her, a few years younger. Their voices can be heard from the parking lot. When she marries, she'll break her lease and move into her husband's house, same as I did, but no matter what happens she'll stay married. She'll get pregnant and won't miscarry and the baby will look like them.

I look around the room, which is bright and large. The sun makes angles on the walls and I think, *All of this is mine.*

After my sister leaves, I take the bottle of vodka out of the freezer and pour some into a cup with lots of ice and a little bit of cranberry juice. My anxiety can usually be tamed with a cheeseburger and fries but I wasn't able to enjoy my food like I normally do, not like I do when I'm alone. I take my drink outside to the picnic table. From here I can see everything—my house and driveway, my car and lawn mower and trash cans: one for recycling and one for garbage. I can never remember what days the trash comes so I have to watch my neighbors, wheel the cans out to the curb when they do. I've met a few of them but I'm bad with names so I write them down on the notepad next to the refrigerator: Nicole and Shane; Ellie and Bill Tucker; Mr. Gorrell. I like to hold up a hand as I call their names from a distance, as if we might be neighborly. Some guys I haven't met live in the house on the corner. When they have band practice, I sit outside and listen. They're the only ones I might want to know.

When my drink is gone, I go inside and make another, walk around looking at my things as if I'm seeing them through my sister's eyes. When I drink, I can't do anything but wander my house, wondering how people live. What they do with themselves. There are paintings on the walls, not just prints. The kitchen is full of wedding loot—nice dishes and Calphalon pots, an espresso machine, a KitchenAid mixer—everything a person might want. In the foyer, there are family photographs on the table spanning generations of people who aren't mine. The earliest photograph I have of myself was taken the day I was adopted. I was three. My father is holding me and I look tired and rumpled in a lace dress and leather shoes—all white like I'm about to be baptized. My sister was adopted a year later, as a newborn. The nurse took her from her birth mother and placed her in my mother's arms and my parents cried so hard I thought something was wrong with her but we were going to have to keep her anyway.

I used to tell people I was adopted from an orphanage, that

I would save paper napkins from meals and make bows for my hair so that when the couples came on Sunday afternoons, I'd look like I wanted it more than the others. I'd tell them they lined us up like they do at whorehouses, and we'd put on different personas, try different tactics to make them choose us. The truth is I don't remember my life before. My memories begin with my sister.

When my mother placed her in my arms, she was sleeping. *This is your sister, Elizabeth,* my father said. *Now our family is complete,* my mother said. And then it was Christmas.

I curl up on the couch and the cat situates herself on my legs. She closes her eyes and I close mine. When I open them and check my phone, two hours have passed. I wish my sister was here, or I'd gone with her, but then I hear the key in the lock and she comes in calling my name, followed by Leah and two girls I've never seen before.

"We were at a bar, like, three blocks from here," my sister says, "and we decided you had to come with us."

The pretty dark-haired girl is wearing a low-cut shirt; my eyes stop at her breasts.

"Come with us," Leah says.

"You're coming," my sister says. "Get dressed, we're going downtown."

The air is full of perfume and energy and I don't want to go but they act like I don't have a choice and this is what I need in order to be motivated. Now there are five of us, and we could all be traipsing drunkenly down the alley, holding each other up, laughing.

In my room, the cat is curled on my pillow. I didn't see her move from the couch. She looks up at me with her big eyes and meows.

"What do you want, kitty?" I ask. She continues meowing so I go through the list—food, water, litter box. I only know these three things. "I won't be gone long. And I won't get drunk, I promise." She doesn't like it when I'm drunk. Perhaps, if I were drunk more often, she wouldn't like it if I were sober. She's a nice cat, and even though she follows me around and lies on my legs at night, I still imagine her clawing my face in my sleep.

I put on the dress and sweater I wear when I need to put on something in a hurry. The dress makes my waist look small and my breasts look large and the sweater is soft and comfortable.

My sister finds me in the bathroom. "You look nice," she says, touching a sleeve.

"Do I need blush?"

"Mascara."

"I don't like mascara. I can feel my eyelashes when I wear it." I apply lipstick while she watches. I've only recently begun to wear makeup and a little bit of jewelry. They don't feel ridiculous on me like they used to, like I was a girl trying to be a woman.

"What about these shoes?" I ask. "I just got them."

"I don't know," she says. "Gladiators are tough. I think they should only be worn by very thin, very tall people. I don't know," she says again. "What else do you have? Give me options."

"I'll wear my boots."

"Wear them if you like them. Your cat isn't very friendly."

"She's friendly with me."

"I didn't know you liked cats."

"I don't."

"So why'd you get one?"

"I wanted a pet and a dog seemed like too big a commitment."

"But dogs are so much better," she says, turning off the light. "Dogs come when you call them."

"That's the allure of a cat," I say, "they're independent," which is what I've heard cat people say. I still don't understand how cats work. You can't yell at them or punish them like you can with a dog.

I follow my sister into the kitchen where the girls are opening cabinets, peering out the windows into the dark.

Leah bends down to pet my cat, bracelets jangling. "I like him," she says. "He's nice."

"She."

"She's a sweetie. *Aren't you a sweetie?*"

"Let's go," my sister says.

I turn on the porch light, lock the door, and we pile into a small yellow car. Leah is on one side of me and a girl named Jenna is on the other. I can feel myself becoming more and more uncomfortable but my sister catches my eye in the mirror and I think, *Everything is fine, everything is just fine.* I try to convince myself this is fun, that this is what people do—they go out and drink with their girlfriends and have fun. They meet men. They take shots and lose themselves in the night. But then the cars on the interstate come to a standstill and my breathing becomes more and more labored and I can't see whether it's a wreck or what. I don't know why I had to be in the middle, my arms and legs touching people.

By the time we park, my heart's beating so fast I can feel it all over my body.

At the door, I show the guy my license and follow them inside. It's hard to make out faces. My sister and her friends slip into a booth and I walk over to the bar and squeeze between two guys. The bar is busy and the men talk over me. I can feel them checking me out, assessing my body. I wait, holding up my credit card, as they talk about a model one of them used to date. I could turn to the fat one and grab him by the neck. I could reach into my purse for my mace and test it out, as I've been wanting to do for so long. If I had a gun, it'd be the same thing. I'd want to shoot somebody. Something would need to happen. I glance over at my sister and her friends and they're all hair and eyes and teeth. One of the guys swivels on his stool, brushing his arm against my chest, and I turn and walk out. I don't look at the door guy. I stand at the curb and lift my arm; my sweater slips down, exposing a slim wrist. I've never been so thin, not even as a teenager. I can see how bones could become a problem. They knock so pleasantly against counters, dig into the mattress while you sleep.

I'm nervous that my sister will find me before a cab pulls up, that the door guy is wondering what's wrong with me, but then a cab pulls up and I'm settling into the backseat. I feel so much relief I want to tell the man to take me somewhere other than home, but I give him my address and ask him questions, engage him in the conversation he seems so desperate to have. He's from Ghana. His family is still at home. He sends money, visits once every three years because the flight is so expensive. Hearing about his life makes me want to appreciate mine. He's alone in a foreign country, speaking a foreign tongue, having the same conversation over and over with people who don't care.

When he pulls up to my house, I tip him ten dollars and he gives me his card, which I leave on the backseat.

From bed, with my cat on my legs, I call my mother. She picks up on the first ring. As soon as I hear her voice, I regret it.

"I was worried about you," she says.

"Did you think I might be dead?"

"No, of course not. Why would I think that? Is everything okay?"

"Everything's fine."

"Why would you say that?"

"I don't know. I was kidding."

She doesn't say anything for a while. And then she says, "How are things with Beth?"

"They're fine," I say, wondering whether my sister has talked to her, what she's said. They talk all the time. My sister only pretends like our mother gets on her nerves. It's one of the things that make her likeable; she always acts like she can relate. And now they have a wedding to plan. It'll be a destination wedding, I bet, and a flight will be required. The last time I flew, I was seated next to an obese woman who spilled over onto my side. Her arms were covered in some kind of scabs. She was very nice, asking me questions and offering me things so I wouldn't complain, and I didn't, but when I got up to use the bathroom, I found another seat. After a few minutes, the woman turned to look for me. She squinted and pointed like I had wronged her horribly.

My mother asks what we've done, who we've seen—questions that are simple and unobtrusive and yet I don't want to answer them. I feel like a child, hiding in my bedroom and hating everyone from behind my closed door. I had no reason to hate them; my family always went way out of their way to make sure I felt included. They let me decide where we went for dinner, what movies we rented, but these things only made me feel like more of a stranger.

"Do you need me to come out there?" she asks.

"No," I say. "Why would I need you to come out here?"

"To help you get settled."

"I *am* settled."

"I could help you decorate."

"I already did that, Mom. You know I already did that."

"I just miss you, is all," she says, after a pause, and I tell her I miss her, too. I wonder whether she really loves me, if she's had to fake it over the years. I haven't been easy to love and it's not the kind of not-easy-to-love that makes people love you more. I tell her she's welcome to visit, but I don't need her help. The cat climbs up my chest and peers into my face. She has such big pretty eyes: bright green, too close together. She begins to purr, a low rumble that grows and grows and I scratch her head, the place where her tail meets her body; the hair comes out in tufts.

"How's Dad?" I ask. My father is on a weight loss diet through the hospital. He has two shakes a day and a small dinner at night and the food comes in boxes and powders.

"He's lost twenty-four pounds," she says. "The doctor took him off some of his medication."

"That's great."

"He's looking so good. He only cheats when we go to the movie."

"That's great," I say again, and it is. My father is doing something that none of us thought he could do. He's changing his life long after he seemed to have given up. Even *he* thought he would fail.

"I have to go," I say. "There's someone at the door."

"Look through the peephole first," my mother warns.

"I will. Beth probably forgot her key."

We hang up and I try to rearrange myself without disturbing the cat. If I move too much, she'll leave. I take off her collar, pulling apart the clasp, so she doesn't jangle all night and keep me awake. She paws at it lazily as I place it on the table. Then I close my eyes and pray, which is something I do every night. It's a habit, like so many things, but mostly I keep praying because something bad will happen if I stop. I say "Hail Mary" after "Hail Mary," which I prefer to the "Our Father." I remember the Protestants growing up, how they accused me of worshiping a false God. I would explain that I wasn't praying to Mary, but asking her to intercede on my behalf, though I wasn't sure I knew what the difference was and the Protestants were never swayed, not one bit.

I think about a daydream I used to have. It started after I

heard a story about a woman who was adopted as a baby. Her adopted family was nice and rich and white and she knew she was lucky but she was half-black and had an afro and never felt like she belonged. She began taking drugs. And then, in her early twenties, she stopped taking drugs and searched out her birth parents. Her mother was dead but her father was alive and lived in West Africa. She wrote him a letter and he contacted her. He told her she was a princess. He said he had always loved her and that she could move to this West African nation and lead it, if she wanted. So she went there and there was a parade in her honor, all of the women of the village lined up on the sides of the road wearing the same dress, singing her name. Welcoming her home. Even though she was a princess, she was too American to stay there and didn't want to lead a poor third-world country. I didn't like that part of the story so I would try to forget about it and concentrate on the women of the village singing my name, wearing the same blue dresses made special for the occasion.

The cat slips under the bed and I'm alone. I get on the floor and try to pull her out by a paw, but she swipes at me with the other so I take one of the boxes instead. There are two of them, full of pictures. I flip through a stack: I'm twenty-three, twenty-five, twenty-eight; we're at the Statue of Liberty, Disney World, Cancún. Having drinks at a TGI Fridays somewhere in Florida. There isn't a single place I'd want to return to, not a single place that interests me at all. I used to research these vacations for months only to end up in the most obvious locations.

I study the framed photograph of the two of us that used to sit on our dresser: my hair was thicker and my teeth were whiter and I was wearing a navy blue bikini I don't have anymore. I think about calling him but he won't answer. The last time he picked up, he said, *Do you want me to have to change my number? Is that what you want?*

I hear my sister unlock the door, heels clicking on the hardwood. She opens my door and I can feel her standing there, but I don't turn.

She sits next to me and takes the framed photograph out of my hand.

"I was prettier then."

"You weren't prettier," she says. "Only younger. I think you're prettier now."

"Every day I find new things wrong with me." I take the picture and put it in the box, push the box under the bed.

"Why'd you leave?" she asks. "I was worried."

"You must not have been too worried, you didn't call."

We sit there for a while, not saying anything, while I use the fish on a stick, bounce it around. Its diamond-shaped eyes sparkle.

"I was having a panic attack. That's why I left."

"I'm not trying to be mean," she says, "I'm really not, but it's always something. It's always something with you."

She's right. It *is* always something. I try to remember a time in my life when there wasn't something. When things were good and I was happy. I never think of it this way—I only think of today—that there is this thing I'm dealing with

right now and once I get a handle on it everything will be
fine—but it seems there has always been a thing and that
these things have eaten up my whole life.

"Hey," she says. "Look at me." She takes my hand, squeezes
it. I put my arms around her and hold her; she was once a
baby in my arms, a baby I said loving and terrible things to.

After a while, she stands and leaves the room, closes the
door behind her. I use my crooked finger to try to lure the cat
out: *redrum, redrum.* The cat spends a lot of time under my
bed. Once, I pulled the mattress off, taking the top off her
world, and she was mad at me for days. I don't know why I
want to fuck with her; sometimes I just get the urge. I don't
do anything that terrible. I just pet her too roughly or make
her play with me when she doesn't feel like it. Sometimes I
switch her food for no reason. You are adopted, I tell her. I
have saved you from the cruel, indifferent world but there is
always a cost. Nothing in this life is free.

THE 37

I had never ridden a bus before, not a city bus, not a bus where you stood at a bus stop and buses came and you had to know which one to get on and where to get off. I had once ridden a bus from Jackson, Mississippi to Denver, Colorado to see the Pope at Strawberry Park. That was the Pope before this Pope and it was a long time ago. I was no longer Catholic, was no longer anything. I recalled other buses taking me back and forth to day camp as a child and how I had not liked day camp, though I'd preferred it to overnight camp. At overnight camp I cried and got my period and made the nurse call my parents to come get me. There had been other buses as well, tour group buses, buses that took you from the airport parking lot to the airport. But those were shuttles. Mostly, I had ridden shuttles. You couldn't get on the wrong one; they were all going to the same place.

I was living in a city now, a city with many buses that could take you many places you might want to go and many places you would not want to go and I had to figure them out because I was also afraid to drive for the same reasons and some additional ones: I didn't know how to get to where I was going or where to park once I got there or if I'd have the right parking pass, if one was required, or whether the meters were active, if there were meters, and whether they took coins only. And I'd just discovered that campus parking was particularly fucked up because you had to back into the space instead of simply nosing in headfirst. You had to put your blinker on and stop traffic and back into the space all without hitting the cars on either side of you or the bikes flying down the hill. I watched as others did this, easily, with horror and awe. A lot of them appeared to be freshmen. Their tags said Illinois and Arkansas and New York. I once visited a friend in New York and she was late meeting me at her apartment. I stood on the sidewalk with my suitcase for a long time until she showed up. Country mouse in the big city, she said.

I was ready to give up and move back home even though I'd left everything behind in a way that would not allow for my return: I had dropped out of my PhD program and broken up with my boyfriend; I had moved out of my house, leaving my roommate in a bit of a bind. There was nothing to return to except my mother. I could always return to her and she would be happy to have me. I also had a father; he lived with my mother and I loved him, too, but it wasn't the same. We had gone out to lunch before I'd left, just the two of us, and he'd made the waitress cry and I was pretty sure she'd quit because the manager had begun to wait on us at some point and my heart had cracked a little. It was small things like this that did it.

It was August, well over 100 degrees. I stood and then sat

on the hill. It hadn't rained but my ass felt slightly damp. I was wearing a dress made of very thin cotton. It was like nothing. It was also low-cut and the tops of my breasts were exposed. Why had I worn this dress? It had been a mistake. There wasn't even a bench at the bus stop I thought I should be at but wasn't sure, only a pole in the ground with a picture of a bus on it, big windows like eyes and a lot of numbers that meant nothing to me.

I was in tears by the time I called my mother. I've been sitting on this hill for an hour, I said, over an hour, and I'm about to lose it.

Okay, she said, panicked. What can I do?

I'm about to freak out. I have to get home.

Okay, she said. Let me help you.

Look up bus routes, I said. And tell me what to do. She was in Mississippi. I was in Texas. I didn't have a phone that had internet access but a phone that could text and call only. I waited while she looked up the information. I was pretty sure she had never ridden a bus at all, not even a sightseeing bus, though I vaguely remembered one in Paris. I was pretty sure we had been on a bus together in Paris, our heads in the open air, or maybe New York. No, it was Paris, but it hadn't been an open-air one. Our heads had not been exposed. I had been to some places by that point. I had decided to go to some places and had gone to them. The first time I went overseas, I cried in the airport because I was scared to go so far away, to fly over an ocean, not knowing what to expect once I got there. On the plane, I stayed awake the entire time while the people around me took off their shoes and slept soundly until the plane had reached its destination. And then there was Heathrow. I didn't even want to think about Heathrow.

I didn't really cry all that much but only thought about crying. I was simply recalling the few instances in my life in which I did; they were all coming back to me at once.

You need to take the 37, she said. The 37 should drop you off a block from your house.

But they all say 37, every one of them!

They can't all say 37, she said.

Well I'm pretty sure they do.

How'd you get there this morning?

I took a cab—I already told you that! But I can't just be taking a cab every time I need to go somewhere.

No, she agreed, you can't. That could get very expensive.

Cabs also made me uncomfortable. Some of them didn't take credit cards, only cash, and I never carried cash. Who carried cash? And some of the cabbies were overly chatty, which I didn't like, but I also didn't like it when they were taciturn or spoke in a foreign language on the phone the whole time. I liked it when they said a few words of greeting followed by a polite question or two and then were silent until it was time to pay with a credit card.

The first time I took a cab I was twenty-one years old, in Atlanta for a Phish concert. I remembered other things about that weekend: other firsts. The boy I was with had taken a lot of pictures and I hadn't seen them in many years—perhaps I had never seen them—but I could picture them just the same. There I am the morning after, sitting on a motel bed in my terrycloth Abercrombie & Fitch dress.

I kept her on the phone. She talked about the lunch she'd gone to at my aunt's house and who had been there and what they'd eaten and who had asked about me and what these people's children were doing even though I already knew from Facebook. They were getting pregnant for the second and third time and buying houses in the same neighborhoods in which their parents lived. The ones who had gotten divorced had done that years ago and were already remarried. The ones who weren't married were opening restaurants or making six figures. She only told me about the girls, the women. I was in graduate school again. Still. I had boyfriends who would not become husbands.

She asked if I wanted to go to a cousin's wedding in Memphis and I asked how I would get there and whether she would pay and if I could have my own room. Meanwhile, other buses passed. They said 1 and 17 and 43 and other numbers that were clearly not 37. I must have missed four or five 37s at that point and they must have gotten backed up because there really had been a lot of them, a glut. And then a 37 came, and, seeing me on the hill, slowed. I ran down the hill and hopped on. I showed the man my ID, which I'd been told would allow me to ride for free.

Swipe it there, he said, indicating where to swipe it. I swiped it. It beeped an angry beep. Swipe it again, he said, slower this time. I swiped it slower and it beeped a more pleasant beep and flashed green. He nodded.

I sat in the nearest vacant seat and tried not to look around. My mother was still on the line. I told her I was fine, thank you and goodbye, which was the correct thing to do.

I learned that it was rude to carry on private conversations on the bus. On the bus you looked at your phone or put on your headphones and tried not to make eye contact with anyone because they were also in a transitional space, a quiet space, and one person could throw the entire thing out of balance. Only during South by Southwest was this not the case. And then the locals were pissed off and irritated and in most places you shouldn't take the bus, anyhow, because you could walk faster.

The driver made a loop where there weren't any bus stops at all, at least none that I could discern, and continued on his way. Later I would find out it was for day laborers, though in all my time taking that route I never saw a single day laborer get on or off; it was just a detour we all accepted without question. *Day laborers,* I imagined us thinking, *poor people,* followed by a grudging acceptance.

Everything except the immediate few blocks around the house I was renting from a different cousin was unfamiliar. This other cousin was working in Los Angeles and was renting her place to me for cheap. All I had to do was mail her her mail every few weeks and water her plants but I hadn't watered the plants yet. I had been there a week. The plants would die. The magazines I would keep. Was I supposed to mail every coupon and pamphlet? I read *Rolling Stone, Psychology Today, Real Simple, Time,* and read about things I never would have read about. I stored my stuff in the guest bedroom and slept in my cousin's room, the king-size mattress absorbing the weight of my body. It was the foam kind and I wasn't used to it; it made me sweat a lot, but the guest room was small and made me feel small and I came to enjoy the sweating.

I got off at the wrong stop, but the right street, and walked. I watched the bus stop at the stop I should have gotten off at. The next day I would know. I was thinking about my boyfriend who was no longer my boyfriend and how he wanted to move out here with me but I had decided I needed a clean break, a fresh start. Why had I decided that? I would call him and let him tell me how much he missed me.

I let myself into the house and lowered the air conditioner, turned on the TV and put a bag of popcorn in the microwave, everything humming and working and saying hello and welcome; we're glad you've returned! I would figure this out, I thought, and I would. I would soon be backing into parking spaces and tooling around the city. I would nearly hit a very attractive young man on a bike and he'd skid and fall but would catch himself before hitting the pavement. He would be angry but no harm done. He would not ask for my number or become the love of my life, like he would in a good story, in a story I couldn't write. I would become a vegetarian, swim in cold springs with elderly people before everyone else woke up, hike up a pink hill in the wrong shoes. I would know when things opened and closed and how to get there and where to park and what to order and I would have new boyfriends I would not marry. But all of this would come later and take time, and perhaps it would take me longer than it would take other people but there were some who never left home, who never went anywhere at all.

ACKNOWLEDGMENTS

These stories were written over an eight-year period and I feel fortunate to have had so many champions along the way. Thanks to Chris Offutt, Lee Durkee, Jeff Landon, Paula Bomer, Vincent Scarpa, Sarah Bridgins, Matt Bell, Aaron Burch, Lauren Becker, Greg Marshall, Elizabeth Ellen, Roxane Gay, Kelly Luce, Mike Young, Claudia Smith Chen, and Mark Jay Mirsky.

Special thanks to those who have made my life as a writer possible, but especially the Michener Center at the University of Texas, John and Renée Grisham, and the English Department at Ole Miss.

I'm so happy to have the support of Katie Adams and Liveright, as well as my agent, Sam Stoloff.

And, of course, my exes: you've given me material for years to come.